EXTRAVAGANZA

EXTRAVAGANZA

Gordon Lish

A JOKE BOOK

FOUR WALLS EIGHT WINDOWS
NEW YORK / LONDON

© 1989, 1997 BY GORDON LISH

PUBLISHED IN THE UNITED STATES BY
FOUR WALLS EIGHT WINDOWS
39 WEST 14TH STREET
NEW YORK, N.Y. 10011

U.K. OFFICES:
FOUR WALLS EIGHT WINDOWS/TURNAROUND
UNIT 3 OLYMPIA TRADING ESTATE
COBURG ROAD, WOOD GREEN
LONDON N22 672Z

FIRST CLOTH EDITION PUBLISHED BY G. P. PUTNAM IN 1989.
FIRST PAPER EDITION PUBLISHED BY WHITE PINE PRESS IN 1990.
FIRST FOUR WALLS EIGHT WINDOWS REVISED PAPER EDITION
PUBLISHED IN 1997.

LIBRARY OF CONGRESS CATALOGUING-IN-PUBLICATION DATA:
LISH, GORDON.
EXTRAVAGANZA : A JOKE BOOK : A NOVEL / GORDON LISH.
— FOUR WALLS EIGHT WINDOWS REV. PAPER ED.
P.   CM.
ISBN 1-56858-097-5
I. TITLE.
PS3562.174E9 1997
813'.54—DC21   97-23122
CIP

PRINTED IN THE UNITED STATES
TEXT DESIGN BY INK, INC.
10 9 8 7 6 5 4 3 2 1

FOR LENTRICCHIA, SPIOTTA, ANDREOU, KRUPP
TO NOY HOLLAND AND OUR SAM MICHEL
AND FOR, OF COURSE, DELILLO
BUT WHAT ABOUT ANNA AND KOTZWINKLE?
NOT ALSO ENO AND OZICK?

FIRST NOTE

There were two men who performed under the names Smith and Dale. Their "act"—which I saw once in Boston, once in Union City, and once in New York—was billed as "Smith and Dale" or as "Smith & Dale." I paid very little attention to these performers at the time, and have not troubled myself since to "look" the facts "up." To be sure, I do not know if the name of the act declared the real names of the two men I saw perform it, or if the name of the act was constituted of names the performers had devised for it. "Smith" and "Dale" may have been stage names, or maybe "Smith" was a stage name, or maybe "Dale" was a stage name, or maybe neither name was, or is. My aim is to say that I know next to nothing of the "stage" Smith and Dale and less than nothing of the "real" Smith and Dale—where they came from, where they went to, if they have gone anywhere at all—save that I am informed by persons who claim to follow these matters that Smith and Dale are assigned official affiliations with vaudeville and with burlesque—certainly, anyhow, with low comedy. I myself have nothing to add. I was a boy when I saw Smith & Dale. I took them to be the age my father then was—and I therefore received their labors as being unsusceptible of making me laugh. But it may have been that Smith and Dale's "age" was "stage age," the result of one of those tricks of the trade theater people are always confounding us with. At all events, I was not entertained by Smith and Dale. Their act—two "old" men nattering away at one another in "accents"—hardly concerned me as much as I expected the act to come after it would—a woman who would take her clothes off—Rose La Rose, say, or Lili St. Cyr.

[G L]

Are you the doctor?
I am the doctor.

—SMITH & DALE

. . . the positive is already given.

—FRANZ KAFKA

EXTRAVAGANZA

"DR. DALE, DR. DALE, so please, please, so hello and so yoohoo to you, Dr. Dale!"

"Mr. Smith, Mr. Smith, don't look now but it looks like I am going to be I all over again—so a fond yoohoo to you right back to you, darling sweetie Mr. Smith!"

"Dr. Dale, Dr. Dale, so speaking to me as a general practitioner vis-á-vis the laity, Dr. Dale, so would you say to me it is going to be just like old times, Dr. Dale, or would you say to me it is going to be just like old times, Dr. Dale?"

"Who times? What times? Where times? Listen, Mr. Smith, suffice it for me, as a man of medicine, to say to you, as a layman, I could not be more thrilled and delighted to be getting entre nous with you again—so thank God and thank God for the brilliant genius which is knocking his brains out to sit himself down and think up this beautiful book!"

"My theory ditto to a T, Dr. Dale."

"Listen, please God we should all live and be well and it should be a lovely, lovely book, Mr. Smith."

"Tell me one book which could be off to a more wonderful start as a book, Dr. Dale?"

"As a book, Mr. Smith, addressing you in the context of I am the doctor and you are the layperson, my statement to you is I could turn around and eat it already, it is already so indescribably delicious to me in my opinion as a professional. But so meanwhile, however, would it or wouldn't it be, as a book, too soon, in your judgment, for a certain delectable riddle to maybe make its hellos in it, Mr. Smith?"

"Dr. Dale, Dr. Dale, would I, Smith, have to tell you what kind of a book would it have a right to consider itself if it could not welcome with open arms a tasty riddle here and a tempting riddle there, ennui?"

"Then get your spoon out, Mr. Smith! Because here it comes, one scrumptious riddle coming up, Mr. Smith!"

"My whole entire mouth couldn't wait for it no more with the watering, Dr. Dale!"

"What is it which when it wriggles its toes it goes ding, Mr. Smith?"

"This was the riddle, Dr. Dale?"

"Wriggles toes, goes ding, Mr. Smith."

"Ding, Dr. Dale?"

"Ding, Mr. Smith."

"Just ding, Dr. Dale?"

"Just ding, Mr. Smith."

"Are you conceivably selling me short, Dr. Dale, or are you conceivably selling me short, Dr. Dale?"

"Mr. Smith, Mr. Smith, what am I, a man of science or a man of science, Mr. Smith?"

"You are a man of science, Dr. Dale."

"So, therefore, ding, Mr. Smith."

"In other words, ding, Dr. Dale."

"In words of one syllable, ding, Mr. Smith."

"The clock is ticking, Dr. Dale?"

"The clock is ticking, Mr. Smith."

"But I could maybe take a minute to go run get on my thinking cap, Dr. Dale?"

"Please, Mr. Smith, I beseech you not to insult me, Mr. Smith—because as far as I am concerned as a physician, so where are we running, so what is the big hurry?—to answer me an answer, you could go ahead and take if you want the whole entire complete book."

DALE IS ON A TRAIN, and such a train, such a train, what a terrible miserable train it is which this train it is which Dale is on, you never saw a train which was worse than this train is, wherever you look it's people, people, where could you even look and not see people, people? So Dale, like the man of medicine which Dale is, is naturally trying to get some thinking done instead of just riding along like everybody else is riding along and not getting to anything consequential—but so what, lo and behold, does Dale start to hear when Dale starts to listen to the thoughts of Dale?

The answer is Smith.

Dale hears Smith.

And so what, pray tell, does Dale hear when Dale, pray tell, hears Smith?

Dale hears Smith shrieking and screaming.

Like this:

"Boy, am I thirsty! Boy oh boy, I, Smith, am so thirsty! My God, no one on this train was ever as thirsty as I, Smith, am currently thirsty! Oh, God, who could possibly believe it what a thirsty person that I, Smith, am when I, Smith, say that I am incredibly thirsty! Oh boy, now I really am thirsty! Oh, God, I don't believe it, this must be what it feels like when you have never been really thirsty! Oh boy, oh boy, oh boy, I would be willing to bet you money there is not another individual on this whole entire train who could tell you what I, Smith, could tell you when it comes to a person being thirsty! My God, my God, my God, until I got on this train, did I, Smith, even know the meaning of thirsty? I want everybody who is on this train to hear me when I tell you not until I got on this train did I, Smith, even begin to know the first thing about it when I heard someone say they were a person which was really thirsty! Oh, my God, I want you all of you to hear me, I want everybody on this train to listen to me and really hear me, now I am really, really first beginning as Smith to get really, really thirsty!"

So this is the vein of Smith's shrieking and screaming.

Constant, constant, it's driving Dale crazy.

So as a man of medicine, could Dale sit there and stand it even one more minute?

The answer is no, Dale could not sit there and stand it not even one more minute.

So Dale goes and gets a cup of water and then with the water he has to fight his way through all of the people on the train, but then he finally gets to where Smith is doing all of his shrieking and screaming and Dale says to Smith, he says to him, "Here, take, drink," and so on and so forth.

And Smith says to Dale, "Oh, my God, God love you, whoever you are, to me, Smith, you, mister, are some living saint, which I, Smith, am here to tell you."

"Don't mention it," Dale says and then Dale goes and turns around and goes fighting his way back to where he came from and is just beginning to get ready to start paying attention to his thoughts again when he hears Smith shrieking and screaming again, only this time it is shrieks and screams which goes like this:

"Boy, was I thirsty! Boy oh boy, I, Smith, was so thirsty! My God, no one on this train has ever been as thirsty as I, Smith, was just thirsty! Oh, God, who could possibly believe it what a thirsty person I was! Oh boy, now I really am first beginning to realize how thirsty I, Smith, really, really was thirsty! Oh, God, I don't believe it, this must be just what it feels like when you have just been unbelievably thirsty. Oh boy, oh boy, oh boy, I would be willing to bet you money there is not one other individual on this whole entire train who could tell you what I could tell you when it comes to having been as thirsty as I, Smith, was thirsty! My God, my God, my God, until I got on this train, had I, Smith, even known the meaning of what it meant to have been really, really thirsty? I want everybody who is on this train to hear me when I, Smith, tell you not until I got on this train had I even begun to guess the first thing about it when someone used to say to me they were really, really going crazy being thirsty! Oh, my God, I want you all of you to hear me, I want everybody who is on this train for them to hear me, because I am here to tell you I, Smith, was really, really starting to get really, really thirsty!"

MRS. SMITH HEARS THE TELEPHONE and goes and gets the telephone and says into the telephone, "So hello?"

Dale says, "Sure, so hello, they always say to you so hello, but do you for one minute think I, a physician, am even the least bit unknowledgeable as to the fact that you, a woman, could not stand it one more single instant until I, a man like me, a man of medical experience, comes over there and comes breaking down your door for you to get you and grab you and rip from your body all of the garments which you are wearing on it, flinging you down on the kitchen floor like the hot naked woman which you are and seeking the pleasure of your tumultuous flesh in all of its longing and yearning while you are meanwhile shrieking and screaming to me for me, a doctor, a man of science, to exhibit at least a modicum of mercy, mercy—but, ha ha, I ask you, would I do it? Because I answer you myself, I would not exhibit it, not a modicum!"

Mrs. Smith whispers into the telephone, "So listen, you know all this from just hello?"

SMITH COMES HOME and goes and sits in the kitchen and gets out the newspaper and is sitting and reading the newspaper when in comes Mrs. Smith and she sits and says to Smith, "Look at you, just look at you, I couldn't stand it one more minute to have to sit here and look at you. What do I ever ask of you? Do I ever ask anything of you? So now I am asking, now I am finally asking. Please God you will have enough respect for me as a human being for you to do me a favor and go back downstairs and get yourself a haircut before all of the neighbors all start talking about look whose husband looks just like a floozie. So did you hear me or did you hear me?"

Smith says, "Forget it with the haircut. I, Smith, definitely as a person do not require a haircut."

Mrs. Smith says, "I just minced my last word with you. I am not mincing one more word with you. I am giving you your last warning. Did you just hear me give you your last warning? Because this was it—what you just heard me utter to you, I hope you just paid attention to it because it was positively your last warning."

Smith says, "Go ahead and talk yourself blue in the face— I, Smith, am meanwhile turning a deaf ear to you, so consider a deaf ear turned."

Mrs. Smith says, "Be careful not to trifle with me. You would be making a very big mistake if you were to make the mistake of thinking you could get away with it if you tried to trifle with me. Because I, speaking to you as your wife of fifty years of marriage, am informing you of the fact that there is a lovely new barber downstairs in the barbershop, so be a darling person and go down there and tell them to give you a nice respectable haircut if only for you to prove to me you still got an iota of love for me."

So Smith puts down the newspaper and gets up and goes downstairs and gets a haircut and comes back up and comes and sits himself down in the kitchen again and Mrs. Smith comes in and she says to him, "What a gorgeous haircut, what a terrific haircut, in all my born days who has ever laid eyes on a more magnificent haircut!"

Smith says, "Sure, sure, I admit it to you the man gave me a decent haircut, but meanwhile who ever heard of a barber with such a filthy mouth on him, whispering to me in my ear from the instant I sit down there in his chair that he did it with this one and that he did it with that one—all of them women which live right here right in this very building. I am telling you, to listen to the man, there is not one single woman in this whole entire building who that barber you sent me down to down there did not do it with except for maybe this one particular person."

Mrs. Smith says, "So what would you like to bet me it's the stuck-up doctor's wife up there on eleven?"

SMITH GOES TO THE DOCTOR and says to the doctor, "Are you the doctor?"

Dale says, "I am the doctor."

Smith says, "Doctor, doctor, I don't feel so good—so tell me what is wrong."

Dale says, "I, the man of medicine, shall give you a medical examination in my gorgeous new medical examining room. So please be so good as to succumb to me as doctor and patient and, bing bang, we will go take a stroll into my gorgeous new medical examining room."

So Dale examines Smith and says to him, "My God, my God, Mr. Smith, speaking to you as your physician, every single one of my heartstrings are all going out to you. What a heartache for me it is to have to sit here and tell you, especially when I can look at you and see I have to take it into consideration what a young individual of age you are—let's face it, a person of your age is not even wet behind the ears yet—but meanwhile, as a man of medicine, could I sit here and sweep the facts under the carpet and keep from you the bitter truth? Because the answer is I, as a general practitioner, couldn't do it, I could not sell you short! Young man, my advice to you is for you to go sit yourself down and see to it you brace yourself against something good and solid, because I as a scientist have no choice but to be utterly forthwith with you when I communicate to you the tragic results of my medical examination of your case, which is you got maybe, let's figure, two, three days left to go yet! At the outside! Tops, absolutely tops! But listen, sweetheart, so you wouldn't feel so down in the dumps about it, I also meanwhile got for you some lovely, lovely news which couldn't but give you like a pick-me-up, okay? The little cutie which took down from you all of the whys and wherefores as to your situation with reference to your insurance? So you remember her from when you first came in here to my office? Like with the nice white uniform and the clipboard and the tush and the tsitselehs? So, listen, darling, I know that, as a goner, it will bring you some sunshine to your troubled heart for you to hear me tell you I, your doctor, am shtupping her on a regular daily basis."

"I COULD OR COULDN'T ENTICE YOU, Mr. Smith?"

"We are still talking as to riddles, Dr. Dale?"

"As to what else is worth talking, Mr. Smith?"

"Still ding, Dr. Dale?"

"You are recommending to me I make an effort to throw in an additional ding, Mr. Smith? So is this or is this not the context of your thinking? Speaking to you as a person who is not a piker, Mr. Smith, I, Dr. Dale, would be willing to round it off for you and call it ding ding, Mr. Smith."

"Ding ding, Dr. Dale?"

"Ding ding, Mr. Smith."

"Thank you, Dr. Dale."

"Who could not give to you, Mr. Smith? Could I not give to you, Mr. Smith? Am I not I per se here for me to give to you? You need as a layman, you take."

DALE HEARS they just put in a new golf course in his neighborhood, so Dale goes over there to the new golf course and he says to them, "Look, why beat around the mulberry bush? To get right to the preliminaries, I am the doctor known to people as Dr. Dale, you probably heard of me, the famous general practitioner who is also the famous golfer whose name is a household name both as a practitioner and as a golfer—so meanwhile so forget it when you look at me you see a professional person who is going on eighty-four years of age as of later this month—because meanwhile I am delighted to inform you as to the fact I still got a swing on me which when I hit the golf ball with the golf club you would not believe it how I hit it, this is how hard I hit it. But, listen, speaking to you as a man of science, I got to confess it to you, an individual of my years of age, the question with me is naturally the vision, the vision—in other words, every time I hit the golf ball I hit it such a hit that when it finally falls to earth, who could see it? So could I see it? The answer is I couldn't see it. So what I want for you to have the courtesy to do for me is along the lines of the following—I, Dr. Dale, will go out there with my golf clubs and will get all set up to give a hit to my golf ball, whereas you meanwhile in your wisdom will use your better judgment and will send out to me a caddy who is a person which got on him like twenty-twenty with the eyesight."

So Dale is out there on the first tee and he is swinging his golf club and is taking himself some terrific practice swings when he sees there is coming to him a man so old and so frail the fellow can hardly make it through the grass, this is how old and frail the fellow is, even though, as far as grass, it is no big deal to walk through, even though it is all burnt up and crappy.

"I beg your pardon," the man says to Dale, "but is it at all conceivably in the realm of possibility that you perchance could be the same Dr. Dale who is not only the famous general practitioner I heard about but who is also the famous golfer who has been standing out here and anticipating the special caddy which has been tailor-ordered for him to come out here and see the ball for him no matter how far this particular ball gets hitten?"

Dale says, "I, the man you see before you, am Dr. Dale, the doctor and the golfer and the practioner."

So the man says, "Smith, the caddy—take my word for it, an honor and a privilege."

Dale says, "Excuse me, Mr. Smith, but red tape aside, if you would be so kind as to do me the courtesy of telling me how old of a gentleman you might happen in your own right to be? Because I would not want to insult your intelligence to your face by tiptoeing around the bush with you on tender feet with you, but if I could speak to you, Mr. Smith, as a man of medicine and as one gentleman to another, it behooves me to make a clean breast of the facts with you when I tell you that as to the question of the golf ball, when I hit it I give it such a terrific smack that who could pinpoint it as to where it comes to rest back on the earth again if this person happens to be an individual which does not have the full faculties of his vision intact! So do I make myself clear with you or do I make myself clear with you?"

Smith says, "Dr. Dale, please, let us not inflict an embarrassment on one another with any mutual ignorance of the relative facts—because when I, Smith, a man of ninety-three years of age, stand here before you and advise you that you could go ahead and forget it as regards the afore-mentioned subject of vision, please believe me, I do not, speaking to you as a layman, want to bring about an injury to the slightest facet of your personal feelings. On the other hand, Dr. Dale, here, in a nutshell, is my answer to you as one person to another—hit the ball! I, Smith, will see the ball! Because I, Smith, at age ninety-three, am only too happy to tell you, Dr. Dale, that I got eyes on me like the eyes of an eagle! So did you hear me, Dr. Dale? An eagle!"

Dale says, "All kidding aside, Mr. Smith, you would not be making an attempt to pull the leg of a man of medicine, would you, Mr. Smith?"

Smith says, "Even better than an eagle, Dr. Dale! Even better! Because let us just say like the eyes like instead like an Indian! And you could go ahead and name me any Indian! Believe me, you could even name me any two Indi-ans it pleases you to name me! So I beg you to quit it already with the ridiculous argumentation and just go hit the ball, Dr. Dale—because I, Smith, the caddy, am stand-ing here giving to you my personally engraved invitation to go ahead and please hit the ball!"

So Dale goes ahead and hits a terrifically powerful drive, and the man is of course beside himself with worry, the man is shrieking and screaming, "Mr. Smith! Mr. Smith! So you see the ball, Mr. Smith?"

Smith says, "Relax, Dr. Dale—I, Smith, see the ball, Dr.

Dale, I see the golf ball, Dr. Dale, don't get yourself into such a terrible uproar, Dr. Dale—I, Smith, the caddy, got my eye right on the golf ball, Dr. Dale—believe me, who could not see the golf ball? I see it, I see it."

Dale is shrieking and screaming, "Watch the golf ball, Mr. Smith! Don't take your eye off the golf ball, Mr. Smith!"

Smith says, "Stop with the crazy worrying, Dr. Dale. I guarantee you, everything is hunky-dory, Dr. Dale. I, Smith, speaking to you in my capacity as your personal caddy, give you my absolute guaranteed assurance I have my eye right on the golf ball and what a gorgeous hit you gave this particular golf ball, Dr. Dale—God love you, I never saw such a terrific smack—believe it or not, the ball is still going and going like a regular magic golf ball, Dr. Dale."

Dale shrieks and screams, "Don't talk, don't talk, Mr. Smith! Just please watch the ball to see where the ball lands when the ball falls to earth, Mr. Smith!"

Smith says, "Calmness, Dr. Dale—please, I counsel complete calmness, Dr. Dale. I, Smith, am beseeching you, speaking professionally to you as your caddy, Dr. Dale, to exhibit yourself to all concerned as the very word of calmness, Dr. Dale—because you know what just happened, Dr. Dale? Your lovely golf ball just made the loveliest of landings."

Dale shrieks and screams, "Oh, God, wonderful, Mr. Smith, wonderful! Thank God for you, Mr. Smith! So do you see it, do you see it, Mr. Smith?"

Smith says, "Dr. Dale, please, please, don't insult me,

Dr. Dale, how could you insult me like this, Dr. Dale?—sure, I see the golf ball, Dr. Dale, how could I, Smith, the caddy, not see the golf ball, Dr. Dale?"

Dale shrieks and screams, "So where is it, Mr. Smith, where is it!"

Smith says, "Where is it, Dr. Dale?"

Dale shrieks and screams, "Yes, yes, Mr. Smith—where is it, where is the golf ball, Mr. Smith?"

"Where is the golf ball?" says Smith.

"Yes, yes! Where, Mr. Smith, where?" shrieks Dale.

"I forgot," says Smith.

"SO NU, MR. SMITH?"

"As regards ding ding, Dr. Dale?"

"Try not to try my patience, Mr. Smith."

"Art is long, Dr. Dale."

"This is just a book, Mr. Smith."

"Could our book be just a book, Dr. Dale?"

"My advice to you is just don't you dare turn your back on it for a minute, Mr. Smith."

"But could you meanwhile be a sport and please maybe up things one more ding, Dr. Dale?"

"Making riddle ding ding ding, Mr. Smith?"

"Making riddle ding ding ding, Dr. Dale."

"Take all the dings you want, Mr. Smith."

"Thank you, Dr. Dale."

"You are as welcome as the flowers in May, Mr. Smith."

SMITH IS TAKING HIMSELF A STROLL. So as Smith is strolling along, what does he see but loitering on a street corner a girl who is a nice-looking girl.

So Smith says to the girl, "Look, such a nice-looking girl like you are, what are you doing standing here like this like a loiterer loitering on a street corner?"

Lo and behold, guess what the girl says to Smith! The girl says to him, "Listen, mister, to tell you the truth, I, believe it or not, am a, you know, a whore."

Smith says, "A whore, a whore? You, such a wonderful-looking girl like you, you are telling me, Smith, you are a whore?" Smith says, "Who could believe it, such a terrific-looking person like you, a whore?" Smith says, "Believe me, I, Smith, could not believe it." Smith says, "But, look, when you say to me you are a whore, are you telling me you would turn around and go somewhere with a fellow and do it with him because the particular fellow whose name naturally shall be nameless gave you some money from his pocket for you to do it with him?" Smith says, "Because, listen, if this is what you mean by a whore, then I want you to know I, Smith, never heard of such a thing as regards such a sensational-looking girl like you are, who must, let's face it, be from the finest of families."

"Sure, I'm from the finest of families," the girl says. "My people are the Dales," the girl says. "You probably heard of the Dales," the girl says. "You know," the girl says, "the family which has like the medical man in it?"

"Sure, sure, who didn't hear of the Dales?" Smith says. "The loveliest family in the world," Smith says. "If there was ever a contest for a lovely family, believe me, the Dales would come in first in all three categories, first, second, and third, plus also in the daily double," Smith says. "But, hey, so tell me, young lady," Smith says, "with regard to your specific profession, how much exactly would a person have to actually reach his hand into his pocket for, taking it into consideration the person was thoroughly conversant with the Dale family and was also of, you know, of the same religion which you are?"

The girl says, "I get twenty dollars."

Smith says, "You are kidding me, twenty dollars!" Smith says, "You are saying to me, Smith, twenty dollars?" Smith says, "How can you say to me, Smith, a thing like this, twenty dollars!" Smith says, "Naturally, speaking to you totally in theory, who couldn't see you would be worth every red cent of it, but all kidding aside, we have to face it, I never heard of anything like it, a total of twenty dollars!" Smith says to her, "But, look, given the fact I am very close to the Dales and given the fact I myself would not be a bit surprised if it suddenly turned out the Dales and the Smiths probably all attend together somewhere as regards their religious congregation together, my question to you is this—do you or do you not think you could possibly see your way clear to making a single small exception for personal reasons so that, as two civilized human beings, we could put an end to all of this coarse and insensitive haggling—nay, quibbling—and call it ten dollars?"

"Nothing doing," the girl says. "Not a chance," the girl says. "Twenty is what I have to get even though I personally would be the first one to realize if anyone deserves a discount, then you, as a Smith, you deserve a discount."

Smith says, "Hold it, hold it, wait a minute—because in my opinion I think it behooves us for us to bear in mind nothing is solved when two people suddenly go rushing into their various different philosophical positions without first stopping to reconsider the situation from the question of all of the possible ramifications. In other words, let's face it, given the fact that you and I might as well be related to each other, my final word to you is I could probably go as high as maybe fifteen ninety-five."

The girl says, "I'd really love to, but in all honesty, fifteen ninety-five is out of the question, you know?"

"Okay, okay," says Smith, "so do we or do we not have a mutual arrangement at seventeen fifty?"

The girl says, "All right, seventeen fifty, we'll go ahead and make it seventeen fifty—but just so you know at seventeen fifty I am not even breaking even, okay?"

ALL OF A SUDDEN Dale suddenly counts it and he sees that he has got a fortune. So he hops in a cab and he goes to Smith—who is a man who is famous as the tailor who is tops in the tailoring business—and Dale says to Smith:

"Mr. Smith, my name is Dr. Dale, the man of medicine, who you probably already heard about because of how big of a success I am regarding my private practice as a medical man in the medical profession. In other words, if I may speak quite frankly to you as a layman, Mr. Smith, when the question comes to the question of money, I, Dr. Dale, am in a situation where, thank God, I would not even have to think twice about it, you could name your figure to me and I, Dr. Dale, would be able to turn around and sit myself down and write you a check for it, Mr. Smith, without even blinking an eye for even one instant. So do I make myself clear, Mr. Smith, or do I make myself clear?"

Smith says, "Speaking to you strictly as a layman, Dr. Dale, I, Smith, the tailor, promise you I got eyes in my head and could see for myself from the minute you walked in here here comes an individual who is definitely what only a moron wouldn't know is a big-time individual."

Dale says, "Mr. Smith, with your permission, I, the physician, will get right down to the red tape with you and tell you that I am bringing my business to you as a tailor, given the fact that I am desirous of you tailoring for me a suit of clothes which wouldn't have to hang its head in shame irregardless of whatever is the company which it should happen to find itself in. In other words, in plain language, Mr. Smith, I, Dr. Dale, am placing my complete situation totally in your hands with the understanding that, God willing, the eventual result will be a suit of clothes which will know no peer even as to what the king and queen would have on their backs. So, tell me, do I or do I not communicate with you, Mr. Smith?"

Smith says, "You could rest assured, Dr. Dale, that I, Smith, have been standing here savoring you word for word as far as the subject of person-to-person communication."

Dale says, "Then, pray tell, Mr. Smith, if you would be so kind as to do me the courtesy of enlightening me as regards the price of the suit of clothes which you will be making for me, Mr. Smith?"

Smith says, "Dr. Dale, you wouldn't get a suit of clothes like what you want for one penny less than eleven hundred dollars, depending on the question of stitches per inch, which naturally we, as two civilized gentlemen, can sit down and discuss and come to a fit abridgment in due course."

Dale says, "Mr. Smith, I beg you to consider the check already written, fondue? But meanwhile, please to inform me, as your customer, as to the particulars—so, speaking to me as your client, you could indulge me and do this?"

Smith says, "Dr. Dale—if I may make so bold as to refer to you as Dr. Dale—Dr. Dale, speaking to you as your tailor, it is my pleasure to inform you that as to the specifications of the garment which I, Smith, will be only too happy and glad to think in terms of for you, it just so happens that I am in close communication with some very exclusive business interests in New Zealand which got the market cornered as to a certain lovely sheep which when you cut the wool from this sheep, bing bang, it is like a wool which is like the wings of the gossamer. In other words, speaking to you in absolute confidence, Dr. Dale, the wool from this particular animal you wouldn't even feel it when it is made into the coat and pants which, I, Smith, will be custom-tailoring for you as my client for you to wear on your body. Whereas if I might direct our mutual attention to the subject of thread— so speaking as to thread, we come to a totally different subject, in accordance with which I, Smith, am going to give instructions to the long-distance operator to hurry up and put me in touch with a certain individual who is very high up in a certain foreign government and who is in, how shall we say, intimate contact with another certain individual who weaves a thread which, if the deal can be structured along the lines of the terms which I am thinking in terms of, this woman will weave for you a thread which is an invisible thread. As to buttons—well, buttons, what I, Smith, am giving serious consideration to is a yak from Lapland. So as a medical practitioner, Dr. Dale, can I take it for granted you heard it when I said Lapland? Because the very instant your check clears the bank, I, your tailor, am picking up this very telephone and calling person-to-person to the most darling young Laplander, please God the boy will get him a big enough gun and go pick out a nice clean yak for you and then, with the gun, shoot the yak for you, whereupon from the horns of this yak, I, Smith, the tailor, will personally sit myself down and with these two hands, let alone with also all of the loving care in the world, will personally, as your tailor, carve for you the gorgeous buttons for this wonderful, wonderful suit of clothes."

Dale says, "My God, I love it, I just love it, Mr. Smith! To me it sounds like it is just too too très for words, Mr. Smith! But, pray tell, just out of idle curiosity, not that I would dare insult an artist such as yourself with such a coarse question, but what would you say would be your rough estimate as to what would be the total time for you to require so as for me, Dr. Dale, the practitioner, to finally take delivery from you of such a suit of clothes?"

Smith says, "Forgive me, Dr. Dale, but did I just hear you say to me when can you get it, Dr. Dale?" Smith says, "Because if you are talking production to me, Dr. Dale, if what you are doing, as I, Smith, the tailor, am forced to interpret you, is attempting to broach to me the subject of production, Dr. Dale, then, speaking to you as your tailor, let me answer you in no uncertain terms—because, let's face it, a suit which comes from here, which comes from there, which comes from everywhere, a suit which is such an exclusive suit, it is my duty to tell you, Dr. Dale, that you would not take delivery of such a garment like this one for at least nine, ten months minimum, Dr. Dale! So did you hear me or did you hear me? Minimum!"

Dale says, "Nine, ten months! You didn't hear I got a bar mitzvah I got to go to this Saturday?"

Smith says, "So you need it, you'll get it."

SMITH GOES OVER TO THE STATIONMASTER and Smith says to the man, "Pardon me, young man, but could you please do me the courtesy of informing me as to when the next train leaves here from this station, please?"

The stationmaster says, "Sir, the next train departs here from this station every Monday through Friday at twelve o'clock noon on the dot."

Smith says, "Thank you very much," and goes back over to where he just came from, pacing up and down again on the platform and looking at his watch and then coming back over to the stationmaster and saying to him, "I beg your pardon, young man, but the train which you were just so kind as to inform me is the next train, you said it leaves from here from this station every day Monday through Friday at twelve o'clock on the dot?"

The stationmaster says, "Get the motherfucking fuck away from me, you fucking idiot kike!"

Smith says, "Thank you very much," and goes back over to where he just came from, pacing up and down again on the platform and looking at his watch and then coming back over to the stationmaster and saying to him, "I beg your pardon, young man, but the train which you were just so kindly telling me is the next train, you said it leaves from here every day Monday through Friday at twelve o'clock on the dot?"

The stationmaster says, "That's correct, sir. It is just as you just said, sir—every weekday, Monday through Friday, at twelve o'clock noon sharp."

Smith says, "Let me express to you my most sincere and personal appreciation for your kindness, not to mention also for your patience," and goes back over to where he was just pacing up and down, and starts doing it all over again, pacing and pacing and looking at his watch and going crazy and then finally giving up and coming back over to the stationmaster and saying to the man, "So tell me, what you just said, so this is also including Thursdays?"

SMITH READS IN THE NEWSPAPER they are casting *The Tragedy of Hamlet, Prince of Denmark*, so he goes to the theater and he says to the director, he says, "Young man, I am Smith, the actor, and what I am here for is to extend to you the question as to whether you and your peers would please be so good as to purvey to me the opportunity for me to experience the exquisite delight of auditioning for you as regards the part of the young noble gentleperson in the Shakespearean play which you people I understand from the newspapers are getting ready to put on here regarding the distinguished theatrical exhibition of the classical undecided individual who could not make up his mind on a bet."

The director says, "Look, Mr. Smith, I really think this call is really all wrong for you. Just leave your name and number and we'll get in touch with you when we have something that looks as if it might be right for you."

Smith says, "What's this, what's this? I, Smith, come in here all of the way up here from downtown and you got the gall to say to me, to Smith, to Smith, the actor, that you will, you know, get in touch? Smith already laid out for carfare up from downtown and you got the crust to stand there like butter would not melt in your mouth while you express to me the opinion that you, a behind-the-wings person, will get in touch with Smith, with the same Smith who is Smith the actor and who is already forty, forty-five years, going on maybe fifty years in the business?"

The director says, "Please, sir, we prefer not to have any kind of unpleasantness here, if you please. Just leave your name and your number and we will do our best to keep an eye out for you if anything suitable comes up."

Smith says, "What anything! You got some nerve on you, anything! I, Smith, lay out in good faith for carfare to come all of the way up here from downtown and you meanwhile are saying to me anything, anything, anything? How dare you say to me that you could not even impart to me not even two seconds for me to stand up there on the stage like a civilized person and give you just a harmless sample of what I, Smith, am making reference to when I tell you that I am here to take my rightful place as the prince of princes, not to mention the Hamlet of Hamlets! Because if this is what you are saying to me, then I only got two words to say to you, which is be ashamed, be ashamed! That's right, you heard me, be ashamed! Because let's not forget that I, Smith, came up here all of the way up from downtown, so that the very least you could do is display to me the simple decency as to give me a chance to display to you my artistic qualities as a professional theatrical person!"

So the director says to Smith, "Okay, okay, listen, mister—I don't have any time to screw around with you. I'm giving you exactly two minutes to show me what you've got."

But before Smith has read even for so much as all of fifteen seconds, the director is out of his mind with excitement—in all of his life he has never heard Shakespeare so magnificently rendered, Hamlet so rivetingly interpreted. So naturally Smith is signed up on the spot—and that night, after they have had a great dinner together and have discussed all of the profound questions which theater people discuss whenever they get together, Smith and the director are sitting there in the restaurant lingering over coffee, and the director says, "Christ, guy, you know, I still can't get over it, the way you just transform yourself like that—the voice, the poise, the bearing—I mean, I really got to hand it to you, how the hell do you do it, man?"

Smith says, "That's actink."

"SO YOU ARE OR YOU ARE NOT having a swell time in all of these wonderful jokes, Mr. Smith?"

"Who could not adore such terrific jokes, Dr. Dale? These jokes are the most enjoyable of jokes, Dr. Dale. In my humble opinion as a layman, it is a privilege, Dr. Dale, and an honor, Dr. Dale, for any person, regardless of what this person's walk of life is, for them to be able to sit themselves down and to relax and enjoy themselves as human beings who are positively in the picture as to the various jokes of this humorous nature, Dr. Dale."

"Yet leave us not, both as professional people and as laymen, nevertheless run the risk of overlooking the necessity of also, you know, of also riddles, Mr. Smith."

"I couldn't agree with you more, Dr. Dale."

"So speaking to you with reference to which, Mr. Smith, you are or you are not one hundred percent prepared to purvey to me your answer, Mr. Smith?"

"As regards howsoever many dings it should happen to suit me, Smith, the layman, to consider, Dr. Dale?"

"This was my very question to you, Mr. Smith."

"You mean as to wriggles and as to toes and as to so forth and so on, Dr. Dale?"

"Need one say très roué, Mr. Smith?"

"So could you possibly maybe first estimate for me how many pages we still got to go yet, Dr. Dale?"

"Pages, pages, pages—what is the matter with you, Mr. Smith, that you never heard of paragraphs, that you never heard of sentences, that it never dawned on you, Mr. Smith, that the very next comma, that the very next period could maybe, Mr. Smith, be our last?"

"Dr. Dale, Dr. Dale, so do I have to tell you therefore that who in their right minds should ever be so bold as to never not talk in terms of a noninterrogative, Dr. Dale?"

DALE IS SITTING ON THE TRAIN and he hears up ahead of him Smith shrieking and screaming, "Oh, God, am I thirsty! Oh, God, I am so thirsty! Oh, God, I cannot believe it that I, Smith, could be so thirsty! Oh, God, it is amazing to me that anybody in the world could ever get to be this thirsty! My God, my God, my God, who in a million years would ever believe it if I told them what it feels like for a human being to get to be so unbelievably thirsty! My God, if someone ever came up to me and they said to me that it was anywhere in the cards for someone to get as thirsty as I, Smith, am right this instant thirsty, then I, Smith, would have to tell them I don't believe it, I don't believe it, because this is how thirsty I, Smith, am thirsty!"

And so on and so forth.

In this vein.

So when Dale cannot stand it for one more instant, he goes and gets a cup of water and he fights his way with the water up to the other end of the train trying to get through all of the people and he finally gets through all of the people and he gets to Smith and Dale says to Smith, "Excuse me, Mr. Smith, but could I maybe please interest you in like this, you know, this nice cup of water?"

So Smith takes it and drinks it and says to Dale, "Thank you, Dr. Dale, what a sweetheart you are, Dr. Dale, God bless you and keep you and so on and so forth."

So Dale turns around and starts going back to the other end of the train when out of nowhere a big grimy fist with plenty of fertilizer stuck down in under the fingernails comes down on the back of his head and gives him such a terrific smack and meanwhile Dale hears a voice like this:

"Dirty fucking motherfucking cocksucking kike!"

SMITH GOES TO THE DOCTOR.

Smith says to the doctor, "Are you the doctor?"

The doctor says, "I, Dale, am definitely the doctor."

Smith says to Dale, "Dr. Dale, Dr. Dale, I do not feel so good, Dr. Dale—so tell me what is wrong."

Dale says to Smith, "I, Dale, the man of medicine, will give you a medical examination and see what the medical facts are as to why it is which you do not feel so good per se."

So Dale gives Smith a medical examination and Smith goes home and says to Mrs. Smith, "Guess what. The doctor just gave me a medical examination and then he sat me down and said to me that I got, all told, maybe only a couple of weeks yet for me to go yet for me to live yet as to my general medical situation."

"My God in heaven, my God in heaven, what is it, what is it?" says Mrs. Smith.

"The heart, the heart," says Smith. "The doctor says to me forget it, a heart like this, it couldn't even last even a total of three more weeks even at the outside on a bet."

"So at least thank God it's not cancer," says Mrs. Smith.

MRS. SMITH IS SITTING eating a bowl of soup at the kitchen table when, bing bang, in comes Mrs. Dale shrieking and screaming, "Oh, my God, oh, my God, Mrs. Smith, Mrs. Smith, you would not believe it, who could believe it, no one would believe it, but downstairs in the street they got people named Jack running everywhere and, lo and behold, I, Mrs. Dale, the wife of the medical man, just saw one of them come catch Mr. Smith and cut his head off!"

But Mrs. Smith just sits right there where she is with her spoon eating her bowl of soup.

So Mrs. Dale shrieks and screams, "Mrs. Smith, Mrs. Smith, maybe you didn't hear me just tell you they got these men all over the street downstairs and they just came with knives and cut your husband's head off!"

Mrs. Smith says, "Sure, I heard you, who couldn't hear you, you think I don't have ears in my head to hear you?"

Mrs. Dale shrieks and screams, "But you are so calm and so relaxed, Mrs. Smith, how could you be so calm and so relaxed, Mrs. Smith, it does not make sense for a person to be so calm and relaxed, Mrs. Smith!"

Mrs. Smith says, "Who is so calm and so relaxed, Mrs. Dale? What makes you think I am so calm and so relaxed, Mrs. Dale? I promise you, inside of me, Mrs. Dale, I am like a tumult of agonies the like of which you could not even begin as a person to imagine, Mrs. Dale."

Mrs. Dale shrieks and screams, "But look at you, Mrs. Smith, look at you—you are just sitting there with a spoon like just eating soup, Mrs. Smith!"

Mrs. Smith says, "Sure, I am just sitting here with a spoon just eating soup, Mrs. Dale. Of course, I am just sitting here with a spoon just eating soup, Mrs. Dale. Have I for one instant tried to hide the fact that I, Mrs. Smith, am just sitting here with a spoon eating soup, Mrs. Dale? But I ask you, do you think for one minute that when I, Mrs. Smith, have finished eating this bowl of soup, that you, Mrs. Dale, are not going to hear a shriek and a scream like you would not ever in your life have ever believed it?"

MRS. DALE SAYS TO MRS. SMITH, "So tell me, Mrs. Smith, do you and Mr. Smith have mutual orgasm?"

Mrs. Smith says to Mrs. Dale, "Insofar as I, Mrs. Smith, am aware of the facts, Mrs. Dale, we got instead Prudential."

MRS. DALE GOES DOWNSTAIRS and she sees in the street that there are men named Jack everywhere and that all of these Jacks, they got in their hands knives and they are using the knives to cut off the heads of all of the people— so Mrs. Dale starts shrieking and screaming at them, "Okay, okay, but the children, the children, I beg you, please, I am begging you, spare at least the children!"

So Jack Horner says to her, "Hey, come on, lady, go read your dictionary—I mean, a pogrom is a pogrom, okay?"

MRS. DALE HAS A MARRIED DAUGHTER and the married daughter has a child and Mrs. Dale says to the married daughter, "Look, be smart and take my advice, you and your hubby should go take it easy for the weekend, whereas I and the doctor will take the child off of your hands for you so that meanwhile the two of you lovebirds should only be like a free breeze for a change and could maybe sit yourselves down and relax like two civilized human beings for a change without you being aggravated by even so much as a care in the world or even one single like perturbable."

So Mrs. Dale takes the grandchild to a nice shop where they specialize in garments for grandchildren and she buys for the child a nice sunsuit and a nice sun hat to go with the sunsuit and she gets the child all dressed up in the new outfit and then she turns around to pay the cashier and when she turns back around again to get the child, lo and behold, bing bang, the child, the grandchild, is gone.

"Oh, my God!" Mrs. Dale shrieks, "the child is gone, the child is gone!" Mrs. Dale shrieks, "Oh, God, oh, God, oh, God, what am I, Mrs. Dale, the grandmother, going to say to my married daughter if I have to go tell her the child is gone, I lost the child? Because go and believe it, two seconds ago I had the child and now the child is gone!"

Mrs. Dale shrieks and screams and drops to her knees with her hands clasped in prayer, screaming, "Oh, dear God, dear God in heaven, if you got any mercy in you at all, please, I, Mrs. Dale, the wife of the medical man, am down to you on my knees to you begging you and begging you as a grandmother who for the rest of her life promises you she will do not one thing morning, noon, and night but sing your praises to you from every rooftop in the sky to you if you will only in your mercy and your mildness make a miracle for me and give me back the child!"

So all of a sudden there is suddenly a great tumult of lightning and thundering and Mrs. Dale sees the child standing right where the child had just been standing and Mrs. Dale grabs the child and she hugs the child and she shrieks and screams, "Oh, thank you, God, thank you, God—how could I, Mrs. Dale, ever thank you enough, God? Oh, God, what a wonderful God you are, God! Never once in all of my life will I, Mrs. Dale, ever for two seconds forget what a wonderful terrific God you are, God!" But then all of a sudden she suddenly notices and she screams even more frantically than she ever screamed before: "Hey, wait a minute, God, not so fast, goddamnit, God—there was a hat, a hat!"

DALE CALLS UP HIS TRAVEL AGENT and he says to the travel agent, Dale says, "Hello, it is I, the doctor, the man of science, Dr. Dale, and I am telephoning you to ask you the question of what in your experience would you deem it a good idea to recommend to me as a vacation proposition that would be commensurate with when I call up Smith and tell Smith that Mrs. Dale, the doctor's wife, and I, the doctor, are prepared to lay out the money to take Smith and Mrs. Smith on it, the man would not be able to stand it that it is such a classy exclusive deal and that look who was the individual which first thought it up first."

So the travel agent says, "Dr. Dale, I want you to know something, which is that I, your travel agent, do not even have to put on my thinking cap to tell you right off the bat that for the Dales and the Smiths what is without question definitely the hottest proposition as regards the best vacation situation for all of your top-quality people this season is a nice relaxing cruise on a totally exclusive slave ship."

Dale says, "Listen, if you, speaking to me as my travel agent, are inferring to me, the doctor, the advice and counsel that this is what the people of the right caliber are doing this season, then answering you as one professional practitioner to another, I got just two words for you, which is be a nice fella and go ahead and whatever it costs, book it."

So the day comes when, lo and behold, it is the day of departure and Dale and Mrs. Dale and Smith and Mrs. Smith are all in there in their unbelievably sumptuous stateroom sitting there in such total complete comfort, what with the champagne and the caviar and the nice bowl of various different tropical types of fruits, when all of a sudden there is suddenly a tremendous pounding at the door, and so Dale goes to the door and he opens the door and Dale sees standing there at the door a gigantic vicious naked person, and the gigantic vicious naked person says to Dale, he says, "I trust I am not intruding on you, Dr. Dale, but the captain has instructed me to collect all heads of households and to take them down into the hold of the ship and there to manacle and chain these passengers to the oars so that the hideous labors might be commenced and this vast ship be rowed out into open water."

"Wonderful, wonderful, wonderful," says Dale, giving a big wink to Smith, whereupon the gigantic vicious naked person gives them both a powerful grab and snatches them up each one of them under an arm and carries Smith and Dale down into the bottom of the ship where, lo and behold, there is another gigantic vicious naked person walking up and down with a big whip and every time he passes one of the passengers who is chained and manacled to the oars the gigantic vicious naked person gives this passenger such smacks with the big whip it would make you sick to hear it, whereupon the passenger who is smacked with the big whip couldn't contain it anymore, the pain, the pain, the pain, and thus, as a human being, the man emits from his breast such a shriek you would not believe it even if you were there and heard it with your very own ears.

Smith and Dale have to gasp with fear, this is how horrible it is to hear such torture, it is just too horrible even to think about, all of these nice men who are the passengers on such a gorgeous lovely cruise ship all being whipped like this with a big whip while meanwhile another gigantic vicious naked person has got a drum and a stick and like a crazy person the man is sitting there and hitting the drum with the stick and like mumbling over and over and over again a word which, if you were there, it would maybe sound to you like maybe this: "Stroke! Stroke! Stroke! Stroke!"

So it is not until after maybe about seven days and seven nights of all of this rowing and stroking and whipping and hitting and screaming and shrieking and suffering and suffering—let alone forget it that meanwhile Smith and Dale the whole time never had a single morsel even to eat and not even one sip of anything to drink—when, bing bang, here comes the first gigantic vicious naked person back again to get them and cut off the chains and the manacles and even the leg irons off of them and meanwhile, since who could walk in the condition which Smith and Dale are naturally in, the gigantic vicious naked person has to pick each of them up bodily each under an arm and carry them back to their gorgeous sumptuous stateroom to Mrs. Smith and Mrs. Dale again. So this is the picture of what is going on, the gigantic vicious naked person carrying Smith and Dale bodily each under an arm, when finally Dale is able to summon the strength to barely be able to whisper a little to Smith, "Hey, Smith, so tell me, Smith, so what kind of a tip would you figure it is expected of us to slip a fellow like this?"

DR. DALE SAYS TO MR. SMITH, "Feigenbaum, Feigenbaum, so how are you, Feigenbaum?"

Smith says to Dale, "I am not Feigenbaum."

Dale says to Smith, "Look at you, Feigenbaum, look at you, who could recognize you? I, Dr. Dale, could hardly with all my brains begin to recognize you."

Smith says to Dale, "I am not Feigenbaum."

Dale says to Smith, "My God, Feigenbaum, what did you do to yourself, Feigenbaum? You lost weight, Feigenbaum, you put on weight, Feigenbaum?—what, what?"

Smith says to Dale, "I am not Feigenbaum."

Dale says to Smith, "What is it with you, Feigenbaum—your voice, Feigenbaum, your face, Feigenbaum, your carriage, Feigenbaum! Feigenbaum, Feigenbaum, it is like you are suddenly all of a sudden a whole totally different complete new brand-new individual all of a sudden."

Smith says to Dale, "Dr. Dale, Dr. Dale, my name is Smith, Smith, my name is not Feigenbaum but Smith."

Dale says to Smith, "Shame on you, Feigenbaum, be ashamed of yourself, Feigenbaum—changing everything else wasn't already enough for you, Feigenbaum?"

SMITH SAYS TO DALE, "Dr. Dale, Dr. Dale, what happened to you, Dr. Dale, you used to be such a lovely nice person, Dr. Dale, you used to be such a sweetheart of a person, Dr. Dale, who ever could have pointed to a more gorgeous lovely person, Dr. Dale, so forthcoming with people and such a regular fella with people, so totally humble and mild—oh, but now, Dr. Dale, now—my God, you got on you such a way about you, Dr. Dale, you got to be so high and mighty with your way about you, Dr. Dale—look at you, nowadays you are always acting like such a big terrific bigshot, Dr. Dale, always constantly walking around with your nose so stuck up there in the clouds."

Dale says to Smith, "Who, moi?"

A BIG LIMOUSINE PULLS UP in front of the hotel and Mrs. Dale gets out of the limousine and she goes into the lobby of the hotel and she goes over to the clerk at the front desk of the hotel and she says to the clerk, "Listen, it is my understanding that, speaking to you in my capacity as Mrs. Dale, the wedded spouse of the physician, you will be so good as to allow me the courtesy of bidding good afternoon to you and to your staff of this wonderful hotel which is expecting the Dale party with regard to our accommodations with you which we had our travel agent procure for us and consolidate for us with you this season in your nicest total-amenities situation. So, tell me, our reservation is in order and our suite is ready to receive us?"

The clerk says, "Yes, of course, Mrs. Dale, your room is ready for you, and may I say how lovely it is for us to have you with us and may I extend the greetings of the hotel?"

Mrs. Dale says, "Please do."

The clerk says, "And as to luggage, Mrs. Dale, might I send out a bellboy to collect your grips?"

Mrs. Dale says, "Listen, as to the question of what we dragged here with us, we will get to this when the time comes. First and foremost, what I meanwhile want is for you, as the desk clerk of this establishment, to do is to send out instead of the one bellboy send at least six with your personal instructions for them to go out and look in the back of my limousine and get my husband, Dr. Dale, the man of medical science, and pick the doctor up and carry the doctor in here into the lobby and then keep carrying the doctor until they get him up in the elevator to our lavish accommodations as regards our rooms."

The desk clerk says, "You dirty fucking stinking fucking goddamn fucking kikes all fucking make me fucking sick to my fucking goddamn kike-hating stomach."

Mrs. Dale says, "So you will send to the limosine?"

The desk clerk says, "Delighted to be of service to you, Mrs. Dale." The desk clerk says, "And speaking for the entire staff and myself, Mrs. Dale, may I prove to be so impetuous as to offer the thought that we are all of us wretchedly sorry to see the doctor cannot walk?"

Mrs. Dale says, "Listen, should I have to tell you thank God the man doesn't have to?"

MRS. SMITH HEARS THE TELEPHONE RING and she goes and picks it up and she says into the telephone, "Hello?"

It's not Dale.

It's somebody else.

It says, "You are a goddamn stinking fucking kike and you better be goddamn fucking well aware of the fact the day is fucking going to come when we are going to fucking come and fucking cut your fucking head off."

Mrs. Smith says, "So you know all this from just hello?"

THE LITTLE WINDOW between the two boxes opens up and the priest says, "Yes?"

Dale, who is in the other box, says, "Listen, not for one minute am I ashamed to tell you my name is Dale, Dr. Dale, the medical practitioner who is known throughout the whole entire profession of medicine as a man of science. Whereas to the further particulars, just wait until you hear this—a month ago my nurse says to me just look at me, she never saw me look so terrible, she never in all of her years of working for me as a medical man ever had to come to terms with the fact I was so down in the doldrums and so completely exhausted. So, bing bang, the woman says to me for me to use the brains God gave me and hurry up and go get myself booked on a cruise before I, Dr. Dale, experience what we scientific people make reference to as a nervous breakdown with terrible complications. Naturally, it's my nurse who is speaking to me as a doctor, so I ask you, could I, as a man of science, ignore the woman? The answer is I couldn't do it. So, lo and behold, one thing leads to another and before you know it, I, the doctor, am just getting my sea togs put away in the closets of my wonderful sumptuous stateroom when there comes a knocking at the door and who should it be when I go to the door but the most darling little gorgeous creature who says to me she can't wait for her to be my own personal recreation director assigned exclusively to me and to no one but me from one end of the cruise to the other, the upshot of which, as I know I don't have to tell you, being that I, Dr. Dale, the general practitioner, a person of some eighty-some-odd years of age, am shtupping and shtupping with this gorgeous terrific creature from when the instant from when the ship leaves the dock to the instant it gets back three, four, five times a day like animals, like animals, I tell you, like a pair of wild animals!"

The priest says, "Pardon me for interrupting, Dr. Dale, but you wouldn't happen to be Jewish, would you?"

Dale says, "Sure, I am Jewish. Of course, I am Jewish. What else would I be but Jewish?"

The priest says, "Well, inasmuch as you're Jewish, don't you think you ought to be telling all of this to your rabbi?"

Dale says, "Imbecile, so what makes you think I didn't tell the rabbi already?" Dale says, "Idiot, of course I told the rabbi already!" Dale says, "Moron, I am telling everybody!"

SMITH RACES UP THE STEPS of the synagogue. Smith shrieks and screams to the man who is standing there at the door of the synagogue. Smith shrieks, "Oh, my God, listen, listen, I am not unaware of the fact it is the highest of the high holy days, but I have got to hurry up and get inside to go tell Dr. Dale, the doctor, that his beloved mother, the loveliest and most darling creature of all maternal creatures, just swallowed the wrong way and is choking to death on like a little sip of water! So stand aside, young man, stand aside, time could not be more of the essence!"

"Nothing doing, pal," says the guard. "Are you kidding?" says the guard. "Hey, buddy, you could not possibly be serious," says the guard. "I mean, nobody but nobody gets past me without the man has got himself a ticket."

"Of course, of course!" shrieks Smith. "Believe me, I already explained it to you I am in one hundred percent agreement with the fact this is the highest of the high holy days, but try to appreciate the nature of the situation, what we are talking about is the man's mother, the most delicate and most wonderful of heavenly women, and please, I beg you, do not sell the woman short, because who could conceivably see it coming, a little drink, a little sip, a little modicum of water—nowhere, not anywhere, was there even the first semblance of a warning, no way in the world was there any way for anyone to get ready for it, name me the person who could first think to himself I better go procure an extra ticket in case, bing bang, the woman sips and just from the one sip the woman goes and chokes!"

"Yeah, yeah," says the guard, "my heart really goes out to you, pal, my heart is really crying for you, pal, but the rules are the rules and the facts are the facts and everybody has got to learn to live with them regardless of the situation."

"Believe me, I realize, I realize!" shrieks Smith. "After all, who in their right mind could not realize?" shrieks Smith. "Only a complete and total idiot would be incapable of being able to realize!" shrieks Smith. "But meanwhile I beg you, I beg you, to please make this one little tiny exception for me and let me, Smith, just run in and run out again so that the doctor, the man of medicine, will maybe have a minute to get home in time to kiss goodbye his lovely darling wonderful dying mother."

"Okay," says the guard. "I guess you talked me into it," says the guard. "So, listen up, because here's the deal," says the guard. "You go in there and you get this Dale, okay?—and then you come right back out again," says the guard, "because God help you if I go in there and catch you praying!"

IN THE NEIGHBORHOOD where Smith and Dale live there is a Chinese laundry where Mrs. Smith and Mrs. Dale always take their laundry. But unbeknownst to them, Jack Horner also uses the same laundry—and so one day Jack Horner goes in there to the laundry and he says, Jack Horner says to the man, "Hey, look, I lost my ticket. But I am the guy who has been coming in here for the last ten years and who always brings you five shirts every week—those five brown ones right over there. You see the five brown ones right over there? Those are my shirts."

"Yes, yes, yes," says the Chinaman, "those your shirt."

"So okay," Jack Horner says, "but, hey, I lost my ticket, okay? You understand I've got no ticket?"

"Yes, yes, yes," says the Chinaman, "your shirt, your shirt."

"Right," says Jack Horner. "So like here's the money, so okay, so like give me my shirts, okay?"

The Chinaman says, "Yes, yes, yes, but no ticket, no shirt."

"Right," says Jack Horner. "Sure, right," says Jack Horner. "But like I don't think you exactly get the picture yet," says

Jack Horner. "Like, you know, I lost my ticket, I do not have my ticket, I cannot produce the ticket—the ticket is gone, finished, vanished, kaput, capish? But those five shirts right there, those five brown shirts sitting right there, you just said to me you know they are my shirts, okay? So like just hand them over to me and I will pay for them, okay?"

"Yes, yes, yes," says the Chinaman, "shirt, shirt, but also ticket, cannot give shirt without give ticket."

"This is crazy," says Jack Horner. "Don't you see how crazy this is?" says Jack Horner. "I can't believe it that you are actually not going to give me my shirts," says Jack Horner. "I mean, hey, fuck, man, I, Jack Horner, am asking you nicely and am asking you reasonably just to hand the fuck over my fucking shirts to me, you hear?"

"Yes, yes, yes," says the Chinaman, "but you give ticket, then I, Chinaman, give shirt, okay?"

Jack Horner says, "You fucking goddamn fucking kikes are fucking really fucking every last fucking one of you all goddamn fucking all alike!"

SMITH COMES HOME in the middle of the day. Smith sees Mrs. Smith stretched out on the bed in the bedroom with not one stitch of anything on the woman's body. From top to bottom the woman could not be more totally and completely naked. Meanwhile, coming from the closet—it's coming from the closet!—Smith, the woman's husband, smells like cigar smoke. So Smith hurries and goes running to the closet and Smith opens the door of the closet and there in the closet is Dale—Dr. Dale!—who is also totally and completely naked and who is just standing there, a man who is standing naked in Smith's closet.

So Smith says to Dale, "Dr. Dale, Dr. Dale, what, pray tell, are you, the general medical practitioner and my best friend, doing here in my closet, Dr. Dale?"

And Dale answers Smith.

Dale says to Smith, he says, "Didn't it never occur to you Mr. Smith, everybody has got to be someplace?"

SMITH COMES HOME in the middle of the day because what choice is there except for Smith to have to do it? So anyway, what else would Smith see from coming home in the middle of the day but Mrs. Smith stretched out on the bed in the bedroom with not one stitch of clothing on the woman not anywhere on her whole entire body? From top to bottom Mrs. Smith could not conceivably as a person be a more naked woman. Meanwhile, Smith smells—what? what?—it's like cigar smoke coming from the closet. So Smith goes running to the closet and pulls open the door of the closet and there in Smith's closet is Dale, who is also— lo and behold, just like Mrs. Smith—naked, completely and utterly naked—and what, pray tell, is the man doing except just standing there smoking a cigar naked in Smith's closet?

So Smith says to Dale, "Dr. Dale, Dr. Dale, what are you doing in there per se in my closet, Dr. Dale?"

And Dale answers Smith.

Dale says to Smith, "I, the doctor, should have to as a man of science stand here and be required to inform you as a layman I am smoking a cigar, Mr. Smith?"

SMITH GOES TO THE DOCTOR.

Smith says to the doctor, "Doctor, doctor, are you the doctor, are you the doctor?"

The doctor says, "Let's face it, I, Dr. Dale, am definitely the personality which is the doctor."

Smith says, "Listen, Dr. Dale, Dr. Dale, my name is Mr. Smith, and I ran all of the way over here from where I was to tell you something—so now you know the reason why I, Mr. Smith, the patient, am all out of breath!"

Dale says, "Please possess yourself, darling Mr. Smith, please possess yourself, and tell me, the man of medical science, what it is which, as a layman, brings you here to me to see me as a patient in my fabulous diagnostic office."

Smith says, "Doctor, doctor, I am dripping, I am dripping!"

Dale says, "You are dripping, Mr. Smith? So tell me what does this mean, dripping, Mr. Smith?"

Smith says, "That's right, you heard me, you heard what I said—help me, help me, I'm dripping, I'm dripping!"

Dale says, "Excuse me, Mr. Smith, but I, as a doctor, have to admit it to you that speaking to you as a scientist, I do not entirely as a one hundred percent item confiscate you as to your meaning when you stand there and you say to me the symptom which you as a patient are complaining of suffering from having is that you, Mr. Smith, are, you know, are dripping."

"What do you mean, you do not confiscate me!" shrieks Smith. "How could you, as a doctor, not confiscate me?" shrieks Smith. "Name me one other doctor who would not immediately confiscate me!" shrieks Smith. "Dripping, dripping!" shrieks Smith. "So tell me, how is it you do not instantly confiscate me when I say to you dripping and dripping?" shrieks Smith. "Are you a doctor or are you a doctor?" shrieks Smith. "A man comes to you here to you in your medical facility and the man explains to you that he is dripping and dripping, so what is the mystery all of a sudden, it is such a big mystery suddenly when a man says to you dripping and dripping?" shrieks Smith. "Listen, what kind of a school did you go to to learn to be a doctor in when you don't confiscate a simple statement like a patient is dripping and dripping?" shrieks Smith. "Are you standing there and telling me that to you as a general practitioner, forget it, it is suddenly a total mystery to you all of a sudden when a man speaks to you and says to you dripping to you?" shrieks Smith.

Dale says, "Please, please, please, Mr. Smith darling, if you will please, as my patient, do me the professional courtesy of relaxing your nerves and linking your arm with me vis-à-vis my arm, we will go take ourselves a stroll together into my brand-new medical examining room, where, as I needn't tell you, I, as the doctor, in accordance with the latest thing in medical practice, will ask you, as the layman, to drop your pants for me so I could bend down and take myself a quick peek as to per se the dripping and dripping."

Smith shrieks, "What drop! Who drop! Where drop!"

Dale says, "Please, Mr. Smith. Please do not excite your-self so much, Mr. Smith. Let us not overlook the fact that I, as a doctor, am a medical practitioner, Mr. Smith. In other words, Mr. Smith, it wouldn't kill you to give me one quick peek, and then, I promise you, the less said, the better. So do I make myself clear, Mr. Smith, or do I make myself clear? Because you either got to go ahead and divest yourself accordingly so I can look or else my hands, as a man of sci-ence, are going to be too tied up for me to even think about purveying to you, as a layman, my theory with regard to what is or what is not the modern scientific diagnosis."

So Smith and Dale go into the examining room and Smith takes his pants down and Dale bends down and takes a look and then Dale says, "Mr. Smith, if I may speak to you as a physician speaks to a patient and if I may therefore broach to you a certain very sensitive situation, tell me, Mr. Smith, you would maybe be, all told, as to your total age as of this particular date a gentleman of—I am estimating naturally, I am naturally just making a general estimate—shall we say eighty, eighty-five years of age, Mr. Smith, give or take?"

Smith says, "For your information, we are talking I am a person eighty-six years of age on the dot next week."

Dale says, "Excellent, excellent, excellent, Mr. Smith—speaking to you in the context of I am the physician and you are the one who came to me looking for a physician, I want to say to you excellent, absolutely excellent, Mr. Smith, many happy returns of the day and my sincerest congratulations. But so meanwhile, Mr. Smith, to broach again to you another question with reference to the general situation as regards the overall domestic picture, there is or there is not—on the side, as the saying goes—an extramarital?"

Smith shrieks, "What side! Who side! Where side!" Smith shrieks, "You think that I, Smith, could not appreciate the common sense of a certain situation vis-à-vis the extramarital!" Smith shrieks, "Believe me, I, Smith, definitely was not born yesterday when it comes to one thing and another thing as far as the brains of an extramarital!"

Dale says, "Good, good, good—we are making progress and I say to you so far, so good, Mr. Smith."

Smith shrieks, "And for your information, doctor, I just come from there!" Smith shrieks, "For your information, doctor, I just this minute twenty, thirty minutes ago just ran to you all of the way from there!"

Dale says, "Wonderful, wonderful, wonderful, Mr. Smith—speaking to you as your practitioner, Mr. Smith, I, Dr. Dale, wish to express to you the scientific opinion that, in my opinion, this is wonderful, Mr. Smith! So now listen," Dale says, "my enlightened advice to you, Mr. Smith, is for you to leave your pants right down there where they are and tell me the lucky creature's telephone number so that I, as your physician, can telephone this individual right this instant and tell her to hop in a taxi and hurry up over here, Mr. Smith—because, in all honesty, talking to you strictly as a medical man, Mr. Smith, I would have to say to you that I am somewhere between sixty percent to seventy percent convinced you are just starting to like really get going having what they are having when they scream I'm coming, I'm coming!"

SMITH GOES TO THE DOCTOR. Smith says to him, he says to the doctor, "So are you the doctor?"

The doctor says to Smith, "I am the doctor."

Smith says, "Doctor, doctor, I got a worm!"

Dale says, "You got a worm?"

Smith says, "I, Smith, got a worm."

Dale says, "Mr. Smith, Mr. Smith, quick, hurry, take down your pants and bend over and expose to me your tookis, Mr. Smith, because I, Dale, got here a special setup which is all set up to go for you as regards persons with this particular bodily affliction which you just came into me here with—namely, in medical terminology, a worm."

So Smith drops his pants and bends over—and Dale says, "Good, good, so speaking to you as your personal physician, Mr. Smith, the first thing which we do is we take like an ordinary hard-boiled egg and we make sure that this particular hard-boiled egg is good and sterilized and that we got on it plenty of butter on it like vis-à-vis a comfortable lubricant so it wouldn't be like too much of an agony for you when it goes up inside of you and then we give it a litte push and, pirouette, it goes right up you in your tookis. Second, what we do is we count from one to ten. Next, now that we have counted from the number one all of the way up to the number ten, we take like a plain household cookie from a box of ordinary household cookies and we put some butter on it all over the cookie and then this too we also give it like a little push and, bing bang, it goes right up you up your tookis, yes? So very good, very good, now speaking to you as my patient, take it easy awhile and rest and relax here awhile, whereas I, Dale, the physician, will go away and come back to you in half an hour and, as a man of science, I will at that particular time be ready to resume for you your therapeutic treatment for you."

So Dale goes away for a half hour and then he comes back and he says to Smith, "Good, good, so first we make sure we got enough butter all over the second hard-boiled egg and then we give it like a little gentle push, yes? Next, we go ahead and count all of the numbers from one to ten. So one, so two, so three, so four—all of the way up to ten. So then, now that I, Dale, the doctor, have counted the numbers which you just heard me count from one up to ten, what we do next is we get another nice cookie coated with a good coat of butter all over it and then this too, ultra pirouette, we also insert it right up into the rectum as per the same way we did it hither and thither with the first one, yes? So that's it, that's it," Dale says. "And if you will please to be so good as to excuse me for another half hour and then, when this amount of time has been duly consummated, just like before, I, Dale, the practitioner, will come right back here to you and continue for you the special therapeutic treatment I got for you as regards the tragedy of the worm."

So when Dale comes back, Smith says to Dale, "Doctor, doctor, I got to admit something to you—which is that while you were out of the room on your professional affairs, I, Smith, as a layperson, could not help but notice you got there on the table not just a bowl of hard-boiled eggs and not just a box of delicious household cookies but also like a big hammer—so am I right or am I right, Dr. Dale?"

Dale says, "Mr. Smith, Mr. Smith, so tell me, please, so who is the doctor and who is the patient?"

Smith says, "Sure, sure, I realize, I realize, but listen, doctor, I got to admit it to you, it makes me, as a layperson, a little bit scared, a thing like a big hammer—unless it is your statement to me that you, Dr. Dale, are absolutely positive in your mind that as regards the correct medical treatment for my situation you, as my physician, definitely not are going to find it therapeutically necessary to employ the use of this big hammer, Dr. Dale. So is this or is this not your statement to me as your patient, Dr. Dale?"

Dale says, "Mr. Smith, Mr. Smith, am I or am I not, as far as the two of us, the professional doctor, Mr. Smith?"

Smith says, "You are the doctor, Dr. Dale."

Dale says, "In other words, when you, as the patient, came to me, as the doctor, to be the doctor for you to take

care of the worm in you, Mr. Smith, believe me, you came
to the medical practitioner which got himself like a one
hundred percent methodology for him to do it, bar none."

Smith says, "God bless you and keep you, Dr. Dale—
because I, as a layman, hate to think what would happen to
people like me if an individual such as yourself was not in
the business of practicing the medical profession."

"Excellent, excellent," says Dale, "but now speaking to you
in the context that you are creating a derivation and interrupting the treatment, please to just be calm and relaxed and
bend all of the way over again while I, acting as your physician, pray continue. Now then, first and foremost, there is
the buttering and the inserting of the hard-boiled egg, yes?
Then, like before, we count from one to ten. So finally this
brings us to the final step, which is the buttered cookie—so
we give another buttered cookie a nice gentle little push and,
bing bang, up it goes right up into the afflicted tookis, yes?"

So from the time when he first comes in into Dale's
office in the morning, this is the situation with Smith and
his worm—over and over again, the man has to be there all
bent over like this with his pants down and every half hour
Dale comes back into the treatment room and gives Smith
the same treatment until Smith could not conceivably stand
it no more and he shrieks—he shrieks, "Doctor, doctor—I,
Smith, your patient, could not stand it in my mind no more
to bend over like this and be naked no more!"

Dale says, "Take it easy, relax, I promise you, this one

here, I give you my written guarantee, is definitely the last treatment. With this last final medical treatment here, I, Dale, as a man of science, am only too happy and glad to tell you, the worm is definitely finished, it's curtains."

So Smith bends over and Dale butters another hard-boiled egg and gives it just the right push and it goes right up Smith's tookis. Then Dale picks up the hammer and starts counting—he counts, "So one, so two, so three, so four," and so on and so forth. But after Dale gets to ten, he just keeps on going—he counts, "So eleven, so twelve . . ."

Smith shrieks, "Doctor, doctor, I can't take it no more—you're killing me, you are killing me—my back, my naked-ness, my embarrassment, please, please!"

Dale says, "I am asking you, Mr. Smith, to possess your-self, Mr. Smith—so sixteen, so seventeen . . ."

Smith shrieks, "I beg you, I beg you, doctor, doctor, quit it, please quit it—two more seconds of this and I, Smith, the patient, am going to have to faint!"

Dale pleads with him, he pleads, "Patience, patience, Mr. Smith—I, as your physician, am counseling you calmness and patience, Mr. Smith, please be so good as to exhibit calmness and patience, Mr. Smith—so where was I?" says Dale, "Twenty-three, twenty-four, twenty-five—"

Smith screams the most horrible scream. He screams, "Please, please, doctor, doctor, I beg you for you to do something, do something—I am beseeching you as your patient, Dr. Dale, please God do something quick, because I am definitely going to faint, Dr. Dale!"

Dale screams back at him, "Hold on, Mr. Smith! Take deep breaths, Mr. Smith! I guarantee you, just another two more medically guaranteed seconds, Mr. Smith!"

"Great God in heaven!" shrieks Smith. "What in the name of God are we waiting for?" shrieks Smith.

Whereupon just at this very instant there is suddenly such a tumult in Smith's tookis and the worm all of a sudden sticks its head out and it says to Dr. Dale, "So tell me, Dale, so how come you forgot about the cookie?"

"Mamser!" screams Dale. "Dirty bastard!" screams Dale. "Say hello instead to this hammer!" screams Dale.

SMITH SUDDENLY MAKES A FORTUNE OF MONEY. All of a sudden Smith suddenly makes an absolute fortune of money. You could choke a horse with it, this is how much money Smith has suddenly made as regards the various different amounts of money which Smith could have made. So, bing bang, Smith decides in his mind he should go call a decorator to come in as regards getting his office looking like it is the office of an individual who could go out and choke horses if he wants to with his money.

So the decorator comes in and Smith says to the decorator, "Look, I, Smith, am a man which when it comes to money, I got it, I got it." Smith says, "Look, vis-à-vis the conversation, don't worry, you could spend whatever is necessary because whatever is necessary, I, Smith, could afford double." Smith says, "So, listen, I want you to be a nice fella and sit yourself down and decide in your mind what I,

Smith, the rich man, should make it my business to have exhibited here in my office, and then you will go out and you will get it and then you and Smith, as the individual who is writing the checks out for you, will sit down here like two civilized human beings and discuss it."

So the decorator goes out and comes back and when he comes back, the decorator has with him an absolutely perfectly blank canvas. So Smith says to the man, "What's this, pray tell, what's this, what's this?"

The decorator says to Smith, "Mr. Smith, as if I had to tell an individual like you what this is, but just for the sake of good graces, this is the modern art which you, as a cultivated person, have been hearing so much about from all of the most exclusive rich people which you, as Mr. Smith, consort with. So tell me, Mr. Smith, speaking to me as an exclusive individual yourself, don't you just adore it?"

Smith says, "Who could not adore it?" Smith says, "Such a totally gorgeous modern art, who in their right mind would not totally adore it?" Smith says, "Listen, I really got to hand it to you, this is the most gorgeous modern art which I, Smith, ever in all of my born days saw—but so meanwhile, tell me, as my decorator, they are asking how much for this in round numerical financial figures?"

The decorator says, "Mr. Smith, if we act with all haste, not delaying by even so much as a few seconds, I believe it would be in the cards whereby I, your decorator, could maybe pick this up for us for just under twenty thousand."

So Smith writes out the check and the next day the decorator comes back with another completely blank canvas just
like the first one, and Smith says to the decorator, "One
thing I, Smith, want to tell you, which is that when I, Smith,
enter into a retention situation with a decorator, let's face it,
it looks like I know what is what vis-à-vis decorators."

"You like it!" says the decorator.

"Like it!" shrieks Smith. "I am totally smitten with it!"
shrieks Smith. "How do you do it, left and right, such ter-
ifically total scrumptious modern art!" shrieks Smith.

The decorator says, "Oh, I am so happy and excited,
Mr. Smith. It is such a thrill to work with you, Mr. Smith.
You just cannot imagine how awful it is for me to have to
work with all of those très, très, très barbarians, Mr. Smith.
I mean, you think any of them knows anything, Mr.
Smith? Because they do not know anything, Mr. Smith!
Let me tell you what they are, Mr. Smith. Can I tell you
what they are, Mr. Smith? Because to me, your decorator,
what they honestly are is just nothing but big nothings,
Mr. Smith. This is exactly what they honestly are to me,
Mr. Smith—big nothings, plain and simple. Whereas
exclusive people such as yourself, Mr. Smith, cultivated
individuals such as yourself, Mr. Smith, it is the persons of
your type of ilk, Mr. Smith, who make my life as a decorator worth living. So okay, so this one is literally being
given away at forty thousand, Mr. Smith."

Smith says, "Please, please, you are naturally embarrass-

ing me—noblesse oblige to you too, of course, of course."
Whereupon Smith writes out another check and the decorator goes away with it and then the decorator comes back
again the next day and, just like before, what the decorator
has brought with him is another completely blank canvas,
except this time, down at the bottom of it, over in one of
the corners of it, there is a little teensy tiny black dot.

"So?" says Smith. "So what's this?" says Smith. "So you
are exhibiting to me, Smith, exactly what?" says Smith.

"My God!" shrieks the decorator. "Don't you recognize
it, Mr. Smith?" shrieks the decorator. "I don't believe it, I
don't believe it!" shrieks the decorator, "that I, as a mere
decorator, would have to stand here and point out to you,
Mr. Smith, the famous rich individual, what you are looking at when you are looking at modern art, Mr. Smith!"

Smith shrieks, "What recognize! Who recognize! Where
recognize!" Smith shrieks, "Sure, I, Smith, recognized! I
promise you, I, Smith, recognized! The instant you walked
in here, believe me, Smith stood here and recognized!"

The decorator screams, "Oh, God, Mr. Smith, Mr.
Smith, what a relief, Mr. Smith—I mean, for a minute I
honestly for a second thought you had just magically turned
into someone who was not so ultra-refined anymore."

"Forget it," says Smith. "Put it out of your mind," says
Smith. "So tell me," says Smith, "this particular modern art,
they are asking for it, you would say, in the vicinity of what
figure as it relates to a definite monetary amount?"

The decorator says, "Mr. Smith, Mr. Smith, a modern

art like this one is, it is an absolute steal at just a scintilla over one hundred measly thousand dollars."

Smith says, "Yeah, well, sure, you naturally realize, as my decorator, that by the same token to me, Smith, it is definitely not a question of the scintilla or not—but meanwhile just let me look and think for two seconds because I did not already yet get myself so totally acclimated to it yet and am, to tell you the truth, more or less a little as yet undecided, if I, Smith, may have your permission to quote to you from the conversation of a certain Shakespearean prince who is going to go non-aforementioned."

The decorator says, "Mr. Smith, I, as your decorator, naturally take it as my professional duty to shield you from any and all vestiges of embarrassment, sir, which is why I have no choice but to tell you that you would be perpetrating irreparable damage to your reputation as a patron of the modern arts, sir, if it should ever start to get around town that you were standing here and looking at a great creation tantamount to this one and were even the smallest teensiest tiny smidgen of a particle undecided about it."

"Who smidgen! What smidgen! Where smidgen!" shrieks Smith. "I promise you," shrieks Smith, "I, Smith, was never even for a single instant a smidgen undecided with reference to a definite decision!" Shrieks Smith, "But so is it such a crime for a total of two seconds it happened to look to me like for that kind of a financial figure, it is maybe, as a modern art goes, just a little too ongepotchket?"

SMITH IS ON HIS WAY TO HIS OFFICE when all of a sudden it suddenly dawns on him that today is his anniversary and that it totally completely slipped his mind for him to go make an arrangement for something special for Mrs. Smith which would be a token of the tremendous depths of Smith's feelings for Mrs. Smith, so inasmuch as he is passing a pet shop, Smith goes into the pet shop and he says to the clerk, "I beg your pardon, young man, but if you would please be so kind as to tell me what you got in here in this establishment which you would recommend to me as an anniversary gift for my bride of wedded bliss, the lovely Mrs. Smith."

"How about a nice bird?" says the clerk.

"A bird?" says Smith. "What kind of a bird could conceivably express the dimensions of my heartfelt emotions for the irrevocable Mrs. Smith?"

"Well," says the clerk, "we got a bird here which we sell here which costs five thousand dollars."

"A bird which costs five thousand dollars!" says Smith. "What kind of a bird costs five thousand dollars?" says Smith. "I, Smith, never in my life ever heard of a bird which would cost for you to buy it five thousand dollars," says Smith.

"Well," says the clerk, "this is a bird which talks in lots and lots of different languages."

Smith says, "It's a bird which talks?" Smith says, "You are telling me, Smith, it is a bird which in various different languages it actually talks?" Smith says, "Okay, wrap up the bird in a nice package for me and put in a card with it which says love and kisses from your devoted Smith, and meanwhile for this kind of money, which I don't have to remind you is five thousand dollars, you could be a sport and have the bird hand-delivered for me without any hesitation to my darling sweetness, the lovely darling Mrs. Smith."

So Smith gets to his office and he picks up the telephone and he telephones Mrs. Smith and when Mrs. Smith answers, Smith says to her, "Sweetheart, precious sweetheart, so did you or did you not get the bird?"

"Precious darling beloved person," says Mrs. Smith, "did I, your adoring bride of so many delightful years of wedded marriage, get the bird? Of course, I got the bird, you lovely darling precious person, such a sweet precious person to send me, your bride, by a special-delivery package such a nice tasty lovely bird. Kisses to you, my precious sweetheart, kisses to you all over your sweet precious person."

Smith says, "So tell me, sweet beloved, do you like the bird or do you like the bird?"

Mrs. Smith says, "Like the bird! Sweet precious darling, how could I not like the bird? I adore the bird! What kind of a crazy person do you take me for, such a lovely gorgeous bird, how could I, your bride, not be thrilled to have it, such a healthy terrific bird which is right this very instant is in the oven turning a nice crisp beautiful brown!"

"Oven!" shrieks Smith. "The oven!" shrieks Smith. "The bird is in the oven?" shrieks Smith. "You put the bird in the oven?" shrieks Smith. "Imbecile, ignoramus, how could you put a bird like this in the oven?" shrieks Smith.

"Sure, in the oven," says Mrs. Smith. "Where else but in

the oven?" says Mrs. Smith. "What else but with carrots and with onions and with so forth and so on?" says Mrs. Smith.

"Idiot, idiot," shrieks Smith, "a bird which is so smart it costs five thousand dollars and talks in lots and lots of languages, yet you, like a moron, put such a bird in the oven?"

Says Mrs. Smith, "So the whole time when I was standing there plucking and stuffing, explain to me how come such a brilliant bird, if it was such a brilliant bird, it did not once ever say nothing in any of it, languages?"

"DR. DALE, DR. DALE, I, Smith, the layman, am calling to you yoohoo to you, Dr. Dale!"

"Mr. Smith, Mr. Smith, long time no see, Mr. Smith— so you do or you do not got for me, the general practitioner, the answer to either of the riddles?"

"Dr. Dale, Dr. Dale, you mean what is it which when it wriggles its toes it does not have toes to wriggle no more because people have got to have what to eat?"

"Mr. Smith, Mr. Smith, speaking to you as a man of science, Mr. Smith, let us not kid ourselves, is there anything which is really a riddle?"

"Thank you, Dr. Dale."

"Don't mention it, Mr. Smith."

"Raconteur to you, Dr. Dale."

"Table d'hôte to you too, Mr. Smith."

SMITH IS SITTING IN THE KITCHEN reading the newspaper in the kitchen and in comes Mrs. Smith into the kitchen and she sees Smith sitting and she says to him, "Look at you, I couldn't believe it to look at you, do you have any idea of what it is like for me to have to come in here and look at you, you couldn't have any idea what it is like for me to have to come in here and take a good look at you, because you know what, because you want to hear what? Because it makes me, your own flesh and blood, sick to have to look at you! Answer me something, do me a favor and answer me something, tell me how you can go around looking like this and letting everybody look at you looking like this? Because you know what you look like? You want me to tell you what you look like? Like a floozie! In words of one syllable, this is what my husband looks like to me, he looks like a floozie to me, sitting here and look-ing like this when his wife comes in here to take a good look at him. Look, be smart. You want to do the smart thing? Go do yourself a favor and go downstairs down there to the nice new young barber they got down there and tell the man to give you a decent-looking haircut."

Smith says, "Forget it with the haircut. I, Smith, do not need a haircut. When I get good and ready, then I, Smith, will maybe go get myself a haircut. And you know what? I, Smith, am not good and ready yet for a haircut!"

Mrs. Smith says, "Don't you dare sit there and tell me you do not need a haircut when I tell you you need a hair-cut! Because as God is my judge you need a haircut! So did you hear me tell you or did you hear me tell you?"

Smith says, "Who could not hear you? The dead could

hear you. Even from on the other side of the grave the dead could hear you. You could make even the dead wish they were deaf from just hearing you so I hear you, I hear you, I hear you!"

Mrs. Smith says, "Did I or did I not just circumference you right, what you just had the crust to sit there and say to me? How dare you talk like that to me! You got some nerve on you sitting there like that and talking like that to me! You should be ashamed of yourself for people to have to know that a man in your position could sit there and talk to his wife like that when all the woman asks of him is for him to go downstairs like a civilized individual and get himself a civilized haircut so that he would not have to go around town making her so ashamed of him because if you look at the man, if you take one good look at him, this is what the man looks like to anybody with any brains in their head, like nothing but a crazy floozie! So did you hear me or did you hear me? Because I just told you what you look like in case you do not, in your own right, possess the modicum of simple intelligence it takes for a person to go figure it out for themselves without their wife's advice to them. Listen, darling, I, your wife, am beseeching you—be a sweetheart and go down there and tell the man that I, your wife, sent you and for him to give you a nice new haircut as a special favor to me."

So Smith puts down the newspaper and gets up and goes downstairs, whereupon it is not even all of two seconds later when in rushes Mrs. Dale running into the Smiths' kitchen and there is Mrs. Smith sitting there with a spoon and eating a bowl of soup in her kitchen and Mrs. Dale is screaming and screaming, and she says, "Mrs. Smith, Mrs. Smith, Dr. Dale, the general practitioner, just ran and told me that he, the doctor, saw the Farmer in the Dell come into the barbershop and cut Mr. Smith's head off!"

Mrs. Smith says to Mrs. Dale, "The Farmer in the Dell cut Mr. Smith's head off?"

Mrs. Dale says, "The whole head—Dr. Dale said the Farmer in the Dell just came in and cut it right off!"

Mrs. Smith says, "That's it? You are telling me that's it? My husband goes down to get a haircut and the Farmer in the Dell just comes in and cuts his whole entire head off— and that's it and that's it and that's it?"

Mrs. Dale says, "Mrs. Smith, inasmuch as I, the wife of the doctor, am able to determine what the story is, yes, this appears to definitely be the long and the short of it, yes."

"I see," says Mrs. Smith. "So I suppose that's it," says Mrs. Smith. "Well, how do you like that?" says Mrs. Smith. "So what you are saying to me, as the wife of the layman, is this is the whole story from start to finish and that the story is more or less over and done with," says Mrs. Smith.

"No," says Mrs. Dale, "it doesn't appear there is anything more for me to add except what I said," says Mrs. Dale.

"So in other words, what you are saying to me, in my capacity as the man's widow, is that there is nothing else for you to say of an additional nature. So as the man's widow, yes or no, is this what you are saying to me or is this what you are saying to me?" says Mrs. Smith.

Mrs. Dale says, "I believe we have, as the concerned parties, exhausted all of the procurable information."

Mrs. Smith says, "In other words, what you just told me were the facts and you don't have any more of them."

Mrs. Dale says, "It looks to me like it's just one of those crazy things as far as the facts of it go."

Mrs. Smith says, "Along the lines, you are telling me, of like the wishing well and the carousel."

Says Mrs. Dale, "This is definitely, but definitely, what it looks like to me as an intelligent person."

"So you are saying to me for me to sit here and take it in stride and so on and so forth," says Mrs. Smith.

"My advice to you is for you to get out the chalk and chalk it up to bitter experience," says Mrs. Dale.

"You are saying to me spilt milk?" says Mrs. Smith.

"Consider it said," says Mrs. Dale.

"In other words, a question of let's face it, life is for the living, let the dead bury the dead?" says Mrs. Smith.

"They don't have the time?" says Mrs. Dale.

Says Mrs. Smith, "So you are telling me this is the nature of your thinking, Mrs. Dale?"

Says Mrs. Dale, "This is my thinking per se, Mrs. Smith."

"So, listen, Mrs. Dale," says Mrs. Smith, "could I, speaking to you as a woman who is taking it all in good stride, Mrs. Dale, like maybe entice you as to a nice dish of this soup?"

LIKE CLOCKWORK, every day for breakfast, Smith and Dale frequent the same eating establishment, take a booth, order a herring, divide the herring, drink coffee, eat each of them a roll, pay the check, leave. So, lo and behold, one morning they decide to make an exception of it and go ahead and try instead the place across the street just for a change—but, bing bang, when the herring is served, instead of the herring lying there on the plate, the herring looks up from the plate at Smith and Dale and the herring says to Smith and Dale, "You dirty stinking fucking two-timing lousy fucking two-faced rotten stinking fucking perfidious lousy fucking stinking kikes!"

So Smith and Dale say:

"What type of a joke is this?

"This is no joke.

"What happened to the joke?

"What kind of a herring are you that all of a sudden you suddenly cannot lie there and go along with the joke?"

So the herring says:

"Sorry.

"Don't know what got into me.

"Something just got into me.

"Infinite pardons, ingenue?

"But so, look, how about you just come at me again with the same setup again, okay?"

So when the herring is served, instead of the herring lying there on the plate, the herring looks up from the plate at Smith and Dale and the herring says to Smith and Dale, "You are telling me you, their customers all of these years, the bastards could not go find a table for you across the street?"

LISTEN, IN SMITH AND DALE'S NEIGHBORHOOD there lives an old, old, old man who is very, very, very religious, and all over the world this religious old man is known everywhere in all of the neighborhoods for what a wonderful, wonderful religious old man he is. Even the priests, believe it or not, even the priests themselves have heard. So a certain priest, a certain very, very, very zealous priest, a fellow who could not stand it for even one more minute that there should be this wonderful religious old man, this priest decides in his mind it is his special job on earth for him to go convert this wonderful terrific pious old man.

But ask yourself, could the fellow do it?

The answer is no, he couldn't do it.

So but when the fellow is finally all set to give up, because he could not stand it no more, not making any headway, nevertheless, as a priest, the individual naturally wants to at least prove it to himself he has gotten a little somewhere with the old man and maybe has communicated to him some of the wonderful, wonderful things which are in there in the Christian religion, so the priest goes and says to the old man, "Look, let's face it, I have to admit it to you, the fact is I knocked my brains out trying to get you to appreciate all of the wonderful terrific things which are part and parcel of the total setup as far as the

Christian religion, but meanwhile it is no secret to me that the headway I, as a priest, have made with you is nothing, in the final analysis, to speak of. So, okay, so speaking to you as a priest, I am ready to call it a day and throw in the towel, but meanwhile I think it would be a lovely gesture if you would at least exhibit to me as, you know, as a priest, your basic grasp of some of the basic essentials, such as, for instance, let us start with, for example, the meaning of Easter. So could you do this for me, explain to me, as a priest, your understanding of, let us say, the infrastructure of the drama of, shall we call it, the pageant of Easter?"

So the old man says, "Easter, Easter—sure, Easter—you are asking me about Easter, you are standing there and making an inquiry of me with regard to what it means to me when here comes Easter. So, listen, what I, as your student, couldn't tell you about the question of Easter! Believe me, when it comes to what the situation is with regard to the nature of Easter, you could not per se be asking a more informed party for him to purvey to you an answer to this particular question! So answering you, I would say to you that we first have to begin with the fact that the first thing which has to happen is that all of the fellows who live there in the village all have to go get their gun and like put like a bullet in and then go run to like the woods and when they get there to the woods they all start looking high and low for the big bird which is in there in the woods and which is making such a terrific rumpus because naturally, as a bird, it is so excited it is Easter—so then, bing bang, all of a sudden the fellows suddenly see where the big bird is and then like with the gun they go shoot the bullet at him and the big bird would not know what hit him and, just like that, bing bang, it drops dead, whereupon the next step is the fellows run grab the feet of the bird and, lo and behold, with the pulling and the pulling, thank God, they finally get the big bird back there back to the village and out from all of the various different situations in the village come all of the women smiling and dancing and clapping their hands and shlepping with them such scrumptious lovely stuffing, you would not believe it, they come with such gorgeous stuffing, figure celery if they got celery, figure raisins if they got raisins, figure croutons if they got croutons, please God it should not be the brand they got in the A&P but should only be like a top brand like at the top of the line."

But all of a sudden the old man suddenly notices from the expression on the face of the priest that there is something wrong, so he quick says, "Wait a minute, wait a minute, hold it a minute, you said Easter, Easter, what is the matter with me, Easter, sure, you are asking Easter, Easter! I almost forgot for a minute—with Easter, what you got with Easter is you got a fat guy, oh boy, what a fat guy, my God, this is some tubby, but even worse yet, would the man even have the brains to maybe tone it down a little with his whole general crazy ensemble? Because the answer is no, he would not have them, the brains. But forget it with just the fact this is an individual which goes around with such a garment on him. Because meanwhile just listen to this—a beard! But are we talking about a nice clean-cut reasonable beard which would not be a total embarrassment to people which would have to look at him, or are we talking about a beard which is altogether in a totally different category? Out to here! Down to there! So were you listening when I said to you out to here and down to there? Because this is the caliber of the beard which this individual would not for one second even consider the proposition of maybe exhibiting a little common sense at last and deciding to go pick up a pair of scissors and cut the thing off! Whereas, excuse me, wait a minute, I did not tell you yet the fatty has got with him like a sack, like over one shoulder this individual figures he did not make enough of a spectacle of himself yet—because on top of everything else, bing bang, would you see this person ever go anywhere without this big like with toys in it sack?"

But the old man can tell from how the priest is fidgeting again that things are off the track again, so the old man says, "My God, my God, who would ever believe it what a dumbbell I am, I myself would not even believe it what a dumbbell I am, sitting here like an idiot and an ignoramus when you tell me Easter, Easter, Easter, and not having my wits about me to sit myself down like a civilized person and give you the whys and wherefores of Easter, which you got a perfect right, in my opinion, to expect. So, listen, erase what I said, just go ahead and do me a favor and pick up an eraser and erase every word which I just said, because when it comes to Easter, in all seriousness, what you first got to begin with is the fact that in residence there in the village there is the dearest, sweetest, loveliest, most charming, darling, definitely clean-cut, absolutely unbelievably well-mannered fellow who has got such a face on him it would drive you crazy to see it because you would think to yourself an angel, an angel, this darling person is absolutely an angel—but, hey, wait a minute, excuse me a minute, could all of the roughnecks in the village stand it there is such a pussycat in their village? Because don't kid yourself, the answer is no, they couldn't do it. So naturally what happens is the next thing you know, the roughnecks, the hoodlums, these individuals which are such terrible hoodlums, they run get like a hammer and some nails and then when they see him coming, the sweetheart which I have been telling you about, bing bang, these delinquents, these criminals, they give him a tremendous grab and they take him to like a stick and with like the hammer and like with the nails, lo and behold, they stick him up there on the stick, whereupon needless to say, I know I don't have to tell you, nobody is made of iron, so to make a long story short, forget it, you guessed it, no question about it, this lovely, lovely youngster, he goes ahead and keels over and drops dead."

This time the old man can tell that he is finally hitting pay dirt, all right, because he can see how the priest can hardly stand it anymore, so excited is he with the recitation.

So the old man hurries on along with it, probably almost as excited now as the priest himself is—the old man shouting: "Hey, so listen, listen, you think this is enough for them, such rotten good-for-nothing hoodlums? Because the answer is nothing is ever enough for them, criminals like this, they wouldn't be satisfied with something until it made the whole world sick to its stomach to have to stand there and be a witness! This is why the whole gang of them go take this pussycat down from the stick and run with him to some-where to find like in the ground a hole. Did you hear me? A cave, like a hole—and when they find it, bing bang, they put him down there inside of it and just to show you what terrible ruffians these hoodlums are, they get like a big rock to go over the top of it and, believe me, don't kid yourself, a rock as big and as heavy as this particular rock is, it took the whole gang of them for them to even begin to budge it just one inch to begin with, God forbid they should not do every mean nasty vicious thing which they can think of and forget to put a rock there before they go away. But excuse me, excuse me, because this what I already told you is noth-ing already—given the news that here it is one, two, three days later when, lo and behold, poof, the big rock goes poof, it just goes, you know, it goes poof and, bing bang, out from the hole there comes this same absolutely adorable individ-ual like new! So did you hear me when I said to you like magic, like new? Oh, God, the hair on this person, like such a beautiful gold, and the eyes, the eyes, such a perfect like heavenly blue! So it's a miracle, did you hear me, a miracle—this charming lovely sweetie-pie of a creature out there walking around in the sunshine again just like nothing terrible ever happened to him and it's all okay—but, hey, wait a minute, wait a blessed minute, because here is the part which is where the Easter part comes in, because, listen—what happens with Easter is if you-know-who should happen to look and see his shadow, then you could go ahead and get out your spring coat and get it maybe refitted, whereas if he looks and don't see his shadow, then be smart and call up and get one more order of oil for the oil burner even if the weathermen on all of the channels swear up and down to you you will never need it in a million years."

SMITH AND DALE GO OUT FISHING for herring and Dale keeps catching herring but Smith does not catch any herring, so the next day Smith goes back by himself to the same place where they were fishing for herring and he sits there fishing and fishing for herring and nothing is happening, Smith is not catching any herring, Smith is not even getting a single nibble from any herring, and Smith is finally all set to pull up the anchor and row the boat back when all of a sudden a herring suddenly sticks his head up out of the water and the herring says to Smith, "You filthy fucking kike!"

So Smith looks at the herring and Smith says to the herring, "I don't get it, I don't get it, what is the matter with you, is this something which you, as a herring, think is a funny joke? Because I, Smith, do not for one minute share with you your amusement with you as to there being even one thing amusing in it as a joke."

The herring says, "Look, I agree with you, I definitely have to agree with you, I absolutely positively agree with you." The herring says, "So, look, what do you say we take it again right from where the two of us left off."

So Smith is finally all set to pull up the anchor and row back the boat when all of a sudden a herring suddenly sticks his head up out of the water and the herring says to Smith, "You goddamn fucking kike, how would you fucking like it if I, the herring, came fucking crawling right up over there over the fucking side of your fucking goddamn kikeboat and chewed your kike fucking head off!"

Smith says to the herring, "Hey, hey, what's the deal here, okay? So how about it, okay?"

The herring says to Smith, "Jeez, pal, could you maybe be a sport and give me like maybe another run at it? Honest, I'm right with you in this, man, I swear it."

So Smith is finally all set to pull up the anchor and row the boat back when all of a sudden a herring suddenly sticks his head up out of the water and the herring says to Smith, "So what's the deal, Dr. Dale is home today with a virus?"

BUT WHEN THE SUN IS NOT UP in the sky anymore and the waters are down for the night, then the herring comes up talking again and the herring says:

"You better be afraid, Jewboy."

SMITH SAYS TO MRS. SMITH, "I am sick and tired of Dale always being the one who catches all of the herrings and I don't catch any of the herrings, so the next time Dale and I go out fishing for herrings and we are in a spot where Dale is catching many herrings, then what I, Smith, am going to do is reach up under the boat and with a crayon make a mark which marks the spot for me where Dale was catching so many herrings, so that I, Smith, will then, as a layman, be in a position to go back to the same spot and sit there and catch my own fair share of, you know, of herrings."

Mrs. Smith says, "Save your breath, forget it, because I, as your wife, am here to tell you that it would not work for you if you lived to be a thousand—because where, pray tell, is there the guarantee somebody would not first get there first thing in the morning and rent the boat where you, Smith, the genius, went and marked the spot?"

THE HERRING SAYS, "I am really laughing, ha ha." The herring says, "All of us herrings are really fucking laughing—ha ha ha ha ha ha ha." The herring says, "So hey, so tell me, so did you or did you never, you people, see one like which was like all over purple?"

THE HERRING SAYS, "Listen, listen, Dale is on the train and Dale hears Smith shrieking and shrieking from the other end of the train—like this, like this, Dale hears Smith shrieking like this: 'Oh, God, am I thirsty! Oh, God, oh,

God, I, Smith, am so horribly thirsty—please, God, I beg you, God, give me, Smith, something to moisten my whistle, please—because, please, God, I, Smith, could not stand it to be like this one more instant, and will therefore drink anything, God, anything, anything—so please, God, please, God—so please, please, please, please, please, please!'

"So finally Dale couldn't take it to hear it no more, so Dale goes and gets some piss from out of the piss bucket in a cup and Dale is trying to fight his way from one end of the train to the other end of the train to give to Smith something for Smith to wet his whistle with—oh, God, it is people, people, people, everywhere you thought there could not be people there are people—and naturally Dale is meanwhile going crazy not to spill too much of the piss from the cup, when, bing bang, all of a sudden this individual with the fingernails—let's face it, the idiot dwells in a dell—the son of a gun comes up on Dale from up in back of Dale and with his fist the rascal gives Dale such a smack on the head that it like shatters all seven of the cervical vertebrae and drives the mastoid bone right back in up against the base of the brain of Dale. So then Dale, the next thing you know, is all keeled over and is already becoming a terrible nuisance underfoot and could furthermore, as a man who is passing away, definitely use a little sip for him to wet his own whistle himself. 'Something! Anything!' Dale is shrieking, which is when here comes, Jesus—like this cow!—ha ha ha ha ha ha ha. Hey, but could anybody anyway believe it, fucking purple?"

SMITH AND DALE'S WIVES have brothers which all of their lives have no use for one another—God love them, these two brothers could not get along with one another nohow—you never saw anything like it, such total complete opposites, two creatures so completely diametric, they are like night to day, one of them so unbelievably religious you would not believe it, the other one such an absolute regular imp, one brother constantly running to shul all day long to always pray all day long, the other brother constantly in cahoots with wiseguys and cute cookies and smart alecks— the upshot being the pious brother, he cannot make a nickel, nothing ever pans out for the man, the man could not even support his family even if he stood on his left ear to do it, whereas the other brother, the operator, him, whatever the man touches turns to money for him, every single one of the man's dirty deals pays off big for him, whatever the man does the man cannot make a single wrong move from it, his whole life long it is nothing for this brother but one won- derful setup after another. So okay, so one day the pious brother could not stand it for one more instant anymore and so the man gets down on his knees and he shrieks to God, he screams, "God, God, listen to me, God!—I don't get it, God!—I mean, him, he pays you no attention whatsoever, the man totally ignores you and runs around doing every slipshod thing he can think of, whereas myself, I, on the other hand, could not conceivably be more of a worshipful person as far as you—but him, him you give everything, whereas me, me you treat like I'm dreck—so what can I do but go ahead and say to myself go figure it out, because not even you yourself God could go figure it out—because even to you in your infinite wisdom it has got to be like a total and complete mystery, a thing like this, him with the works, and me, your servant, with shit!"

So all of a sudden there is suddenly this tremendous lightning and thundering, whereupon, lo and behold, the man hears God talking to him, and God says to the man, "What mystery! Who mystery! Where mystery! You think I, God, could not explain it to you? Listen, speaking to you as God, I promise you, I could definitely explain it to you. Because him, your stinking rotten good-for-nothing stinking brother, he leaves me alone and always goes off about his business—whereas, you, with you it is nothing but constant constant fucking morning and night nuddering!"

THEY ARE TRYING TO FIND OUT who are the smartest people, which religion, so they go tell one religion to send their biggest brain and the man comes and they say to the man, "Sit down here at the table and tell us what is the answer to the question of what is one plus one," and the big brain of this religion says to them, "First, what we must do is establish the nature of oneness before we can even begin to consider what we are talking about when we thereafter come to the concept of addition," whereas when they say to the big brain of the other religion what is the answer to the question of what is one plus one, the big brain of this religion goes and makes sure the door is locked and that all of the window shades are pulled all of the way down and then he comes back to them and he says to them, "So listen, so you will like, you know, like please whisper it to me in my ear what you in your mind want it to be."

Naturally, it was Dale who was speaking, but would it matter if it was Smith? Whereas from the other religion, who they sent was Jack from Jill.

SMITH AND DALE ARE SITTING on a park bench. From sunup to sundown Smith and Dale are sitting on this same particular park bench, not doing anything, not working crossword puzzles, not nibbling nuts, not talking, not sipping from something, not crossing their legs, not buttoning up their sweaters when the sun begins to go down farther and farther down in the sky and it is getting colder and colder in the earth. Skip it, forget it, all the two men are doing is just sitting and sitting the two of them like bumps on bumps. But so finally where is the sun in the sky?—and it is so cold in the earth, so cold. So Smith starts to get up, and so Dale says to Smith, he says, "So where, pray tell please tell me, are you running, Mr. Smith?"

SMITH GOES TO THE DOCTOR.

Naturally, who is the doctor but Dr. Dale?

Who else would the doctor be but Dr. Dale?

Smith says to the doctor, "Dr. Dale, Dr. Dale, hello and yoohoo and good day to you, Dr. Dale."

Dale says to Smith, "Please be so good as to perambulate into my well-appointed medical facility, Mr. Smith, and pray thence enlighten me as to the pressing caliber of your life-threatening complaint."

Smith says, "Dr. Dale, Dr. Dale, my complaint to you vis-à-vis my capacity as your patient is the fact that with regard to the question of get-up-and-go, I, Smith, have no choice but to admit it to you I could not, as a layman, be experiencing an episode where I could be feeling more totally out of the picture, out of gas, finished, kaput, all played out, bupkis, nada, no energy left, no vim, no vigor, I am a person devoid in both classifications, there is nothing in the kitty anymore, the tank is empty, the well is dry, the cupboard is bare, my shelves are a wilderness, I am hitting bottom, I am scraping the barrel, I am definitely down to the final modicum, forget it, it's zero, I'm zero, an inventory which does not deserve even to no more show its face."

Dale says, "Mr. Smith, Mr. Smith, are you prognosticating to me, both as a practioner and as a man of medicine, the scientific theory that in your own personal analysis as a layman, bing bang, you have finally all of a sudden been feeling, lo and behold, nil, Mr. Smith?"

Smith says, "Dr. Dale, Dr. Dale, addressing you in the context of you are the doctor and I am the patient, I have no choice, Dr. Dale, but to make the statement to you what my thinking per se is, which is you hit the nail right on the head. Because, listen, as a general practitioner, pay attention when I say to you not one factotum of zip do I, Smith, have left—the zing, the fire, the pep—call it what you as a doctor will, Dr. Dale, but believe me, it is suddenly, I got to tell you, all water under the bridge for me at this particular proverbial stage of the game. Actually, to speak to you in all seriousness, Dr. Dale, the tragic syndrome is I, Smith, the layman, am feeling completely petered and panned out."

Dale says, "Mr. Smith, Mr. Smith, if I may be so bold as to propose to you the next question from the vantage point of the fact that I am entitled to inform myself of the answer to it as your own personal private physician, Mr. Smith—so you are, Mr. Smith, as of this professional inquiry, let us say how many years of age at this stage?"

Smith says, "The answer I would have to consign to you as your patient, Dr. Dale, is next Thursday next week I, Smith, your personal patient, turn eighty-six."

Dale says, "As a man of science, Mr. Smith, we cannot afford to kid ourselves—because when we are talking with respect to a situation where the syndrome involves an individual who is eighty-six years of age, could we just go ahead and sweep the facts under the carpet and overlook it that first and foremost there is the question of, with all due discretion to you, Mr. Smith, the proverbial healthy bowel movement—so there is or there isn't, Mr. Smith?"

Smith says, "Dr. Dale, Dr. Dale, forget it with the bowel

movement, the source of the tragedy is not the bowel movement, you are barking up the wrong track with conversation
with me vis-à-vis the bowel movement—because, quite
honestly, Dr. Dale, I, Smith, am delighted to be here to tell
you that, bing bang, I produce a beautiful good solid well-
shaped bowel movement every single solitary morning of the
week—like clockwork, like clockwork—at shall we say
seven o'clock first thing in the morning?"

Dale says, "Well, in this case, Mr. Smith, the next thing
which it therefore behooves us as a professional practitioner
and as a layman is for us to exonerate what is what with
regard to the, you know, the bladder per se?"

Smith says, "Please, please, Dr. Dale, Dr. Dale, do us
both a favor and do not insult my intelligence—because,
believe me, I, as your patient, already have made it my business to conduct a thorough investigation of the situation as
regards the bladder and have totally discounted the bladder—so save your breath about the bladder because the
bladder I can personally testify for—as a result of which, if I
may speak to you as the afflicted party, I am only too happy
and glad to issue to the bladder a clean bill of health—per
the fact that there is not a morning which when I, Smith, do
not irrigate, plus evacuate, my whole entire complete bladder by no later than the hour of eight o'clock."

Dale says, "Well, listen, Mr. Smith, Mr. Smith, what
choice do you, as a layman, leave me, as a man of science,
but to explore with you the only realm which I, your

physician, can still think of, which I do not have to stand here on ceremony with you and explain to you is naturally naught but the arena of the context of, so be it, the sexual."

Smith says, "Dr. Dale, Dr. Dale, with all due reference to you as a refined person, you could go ahead and skip it with this particular brand of analysis, because even at the age of eighty-six, come the hour of ten o'clock every morning, I, Smith, have certain unmentionable ramifications, the result of which I trust I will not have to go into with you on a non-public level, even though, as a man of science, let's face it, you probably already heard every word in the book. Dr. Dale, Dr. Dale, suffice it to say to you, who is measuring?—but if I, Smith, was to do it, believe me, we are talking in terms of teacups, even coffee mugs, maybe sometimes serving bowls."

Dale says, "Well, Mr. Smith, Mr. Smith, sitting myself down with you and conversing with you as doctor on the one hand and as a patient on the other, the only thing I got left to say to you is I, Dr. Dale, am sorry but I could not dope it out as to which end is up with you."

Smith says, "Sure, you couldn't—sure, you couldn't— you think I myself, even Smith, could?—a man my years of age who is in such terrific health and yet, go know, morning after morning could I even begin to drag myself out of bed by even a minute before noon?"

SMITH AND DALE ARE SITTING on a park bench and all day long they just sit and sit on the park bench, not one word, not one peep, ever passing between them—until finally the sun is almost gone from the earth and the cold is so cold in the earth and Smith starts to get himself up and is getting and is getting himself up and Dale says to him, Dale says, "Do not leave me, Mr. Smith." Dale says to Smith, "I beg you, I am begging you, to please as a layman not ever to please leave me, Mr. Smith."

SMITH AND DALE ARE SITTING on a park bench.

Smith says, "You want for me to sit here and tell you something which is too fantastic for words?"

Dale says, "What is too fantastic for words? Tell me what is too fantastic for words. I, Dale, can't wait to hear someone tell me something which is too fantastic for words."

Smith says, "What is too fantastic for words is the fact that I, Smith, my whole life long could never come across nobody which could ever guess what my age is—and you know what? Not even my own mother could do it!"

Dale says, "Skip it. I, Dale, could guess."

Smith says, "Save your breath, you couldn't guess."

Dale says, "Forget it. In two seconds I, Dale, could sit here and give you the right guess."

Smith says, "Do not make me laugh. Nobody in my whole life could ever do it so do not make me laugh with the proposition you could even begin to."

Dale says, "I promise you, I, the doctor, would only have to look at your thing and I could tell you right on the button how old of an individual you, as an individual, are."

Smith says, "What do you mean, look at my thing? Are you crazy, look at my thing! Smith does not let persons which just come along in life turn around and look at his thing. Where do you think you get off, expressing to me, Smith, the fact that you want to look at my thing!"

Dale says, "You want me to guess how many years of age you are, then I got no choice but to look at your thing."

Smith says, "How could you do it? You could not do it. Nobody could ever make any sense of it how nobody could ever my whole life guess my age."

Dale says, "I could."

Smith says, "Forget it, you couldn't."

Dale says, "You give me one quick look and I could do it."

Smith says, "A peek, I'll give you one quick peek."

So Smith takes a peek and Dale says, "Eighty-six."

Smith says, "I do not believe this! I, Smith, do not as a human being believe this! Never in all of my born days will I, Smith, ever believe this! My God, my God, it's a miracle, it's a miracle—so tell me, what is your secret?"

Dale says, "You told me last week."

MRS. SMITH AND MRS. DALE are sitting on a park bench.

Mrs. Dale says, "So what, pray tell, is your opinion as a person of sex, Mrs. Smith?"

Mrs. Smith says, "Lord & Taylor's is better."

MRS. SMITH AND MRS. DALE are sitting on a park bench.

Mrs. Dale says, "So what as a person is your opinion of Henry Cabot Lodge, Mrs. Smith?"

Mrs. Smith says, "Grossinger's is better."

MRS. SMITH AND MRS. DALE are sitting on a park bench.

Mrs. Dale says, "So what is your personal opinion of the general situation in general, Mrs. Smith?"

Mrs. Smith never gets a chance to answer.

There is a purple cow in the park.

It is grazing.

DALE IS WALKING ALONG and walking along and all of a sudden he can't believe it, it is too très for him for words, it is a miracle, a miracle, that after all of these years it should be Smith, it's Smith, and Dale gives Smith a big smack on the back and Dale shouts, "God love you, Smith, I, Dale, cannot believe it, after all of these years, it's you, it's you!" but the little boy has fallen down and he is screaming and shrieking to his mother, "Mommy, Mommy, that man hit me!" and it suddenly dawns on Dale—my God, my God—that if this was really Smith, then would or wouldn't Smith have to also be an old man—just like Dale is?

SMITH GOES TO THE DOCTOR. Smith says to him, he says to the doctor, "So are you the doctor?"

The doctor says to Smith, "I am the doctor."

Smith says, "Doctor, doctor, I got a worm!"

Dale says, "You got a worm?"

Smith says, "I, Smith, got a worm."

Dale says, "Mr. Smith, Mr. Smith, quick, hurry, take down your pants and bend over and expose to me as my patient your tookis, Mr. Smith."

So Smith does what Dale tells him to.

But before Dale can get an egg buttered, there is a herring which sticks its head out of Smith's rectum and says to them, "I told you, I told you, didn't I tell you?"

SMITH IS WALKING ALONG and walking along and he suddenly sees Dale, and Smith can't believe it, it's so wonderful to see Dale, what could make Smith happier than for him to see Dale, but—my God, my God—the change in the man!—and so Smith says to Dale, "You used to be such a nice regular fella, but now look at you, I cannot believe it for me to look at you, an ordinary nice sweet plain person all of the years when I, Smith, first knew you, but what kind of a fella are you now, do you have any idea of what kind of fella which you are now?"

But all Dale can do is not even answer.

SMITH GOES INTO HIS FAVORITE PLACE to eat and he says to the waiter, "Look, be a nice fellow and go get for me please a nice piece of herring with a nice slice of onion, not to mention you'll get for me a crust of your pumpernickel, also plus lemon with the tea."

Whereupon Dale comes into the same place and he says to

the waiter, "Listen, be a darling, sweetheart, and get for me a nice piece, please, of herring with also on the side a single nice slice of onion, not to mention I wouldn't mind it if you maybe also brought me half a toasted buttered bagel, with also, God willing, if you would please be so kind, some lemon please with my tea."

So Smith leans over to Dale and Smith says to Dale, "I personally do not think that what you are doing is very funny or very amusing or very civilized, to come in here like a smart aleck and make fun of an individual just because of the fact that this is how it happens that I, the individual, talk."

Whereupon Dale says to Smith, "Please believe me, sweetheart, not in a million lifetimes would I, Dale, a doctor and a man of medicine, even begin to consider the agenda of making fun of you—because for your information, it just so personally happens that I also happen to talk like this, whereas, who could figure it out, that we should turn out to be two individuals who are sitting here coincidentally within the same acoustical earshot."

Whereupon Jack comes into the place and Jack sits down and Jack says to the waiter, "Now see here, son, you go tell the old boy you got back out there in the kitchen for him to go fry me up a mess of eggs and some sidemeat, hear?"

Whereupon Dale turns to Jack and says to Jack, "Sure do pain me to come busting in on your thoughts there, partner, but seeing as how I couldn't help but to catch the drift of things back there, just wanted you to know it made my consarned mouth go to watering like a fool ditch hearing a man call for his proper rations, though I reckon it sure do grieve me a mite to figure I'm going to have to clap sorry eyes onto them eggs of yours without they be shining up at you out of no bed of red-eye gravy!"

Whereupon Smith leans over to Dale and whispers to Dale, "You see, you see, you see! I knew what you were doing was sitting here making fun of me."

Whereupon Dale leans back over to Smith and Dale whispers to Smith, "Darling person, please, I beg you to believe me—I, Dale, am not making fun of you, sweet precious—I am making fun of him."

DALE SAYS, "Did I ever tell you the one about the Farmer in the Dell thinks it up in his mind that he is going to write a book about farming in the dell?

"But could the Farmer in the Dell do it?

"The answer is no, he could not do it.

"So one night after sitting there all night with his thick pencil and with his thick paper, the Farmer in the Dell goes to bed and has a dream and in the dream the Farmer in the Dell hears an eloquent pencil. Whereupon, lo and behold, in the morning when the Farmer in the Dell gets up and goes to his table to get his pencil fitted back into his fist again, what does he see but there on the table a whole entire book written and, believe it or not, the darned thing is all about farming in the dell. So the Farmer in the Dell takes the book and goes and gets some money for it from the people who live in the dell. But then when the Farmer in the Dell tries to sit down and do it again, it is the same for him as it was for him when it was the way that it had been for him at first for him—the thick pencil will not work on the thick paper, all the thick pencil does is tear up the paper. So again the Farmer in the Dell has a dream where he hears the eloquent pencil and again, bing bang, there it is in the morning, a whole book written for him all over again, and again the Farmer in the Dell goes and gets the people in the dell to give him money for the book, and this time the Farmer in the Dell even gets them to give him some kisses along with it as well. Things are great for the Farmer in the Dell. He never knew how wonderful it was, money and kisses and not hav-ing anymore to be any unlucky farmer in any unlucky dell anymore. So here he comes again back to his thick paper again, but did his pencil get even one inch more eloquent?

"'I will go to bed and dream the dream,' thinks the Farmer in the Dell, and so he does, or so at least he thinks he is doing—for he hears the eloquent pencil, yes—but hearing it, then knows he is not hearing it as in dreaming it but is hearing it as in hearing it—and so the Farmer in the Dell comes creeping from his bed and comes peeking at his table and, peeking, sees there a little tiny man sitting writ-ing his heart out with a tiny little pencil.

"'Ho ho, I know, I know, I know what you like being a little man are!' says the Farmer in the Dell.

"'Elf, shmelf,' says the little tiny man. 'As far as I am concerned, go ahead and call me Smith.'

"'Smith?' says the Farmer in the Dell. 'Hey, what kind

of a name is it, Smith? It sounds to me like some kind of a, you know, a kike name—Smith, Smith, Smith!'

"Whereupon the Farmer in the Dell goes and gets his wife to come deal with this sheenie with a carving knife, the punk being too puny for shooting with a bullet."

[DID DALE SAY CARVING KNIFE?]

[Dale said carving knife.]

[Oh, but you can always count on the general practitioner to know every trick in his Mother fucking Goose.]

SMITH AND DALE ARE SITTING on a park bench. All day long this is it and this is it, they just sit and just sit, what else is there for them to do but just for them to sit?—from when the sun first comes up to when the sun is going down, neither person would utter one peep to the other person nor budge one single inch—but, lo and behold, when it is finally too cold for them to sit there anymore and for them not to shiver there anymore, Dale says to Smith, "Smith, Smith, it just does not feel like it is the 9th of anything to me, let alone the one of the month of November."

THEY SIT AND THEY SIT—since what else is there for them to do but just for them to sit and to sit? But when it is finally too cold for them to sit anymore and not to shiver anymore, Dale says to Smith, "Smith, Smith, is it or is it not, insofar as your opinion goes, me, still me, still Dale?"

ALL DAY LONG this is it and this is it—from when the sun is first coming up in the morning to when the sun is finally going down at night—until it is finally too cold for them not to sit there and to shiver like leaves anymore if they still have to sit there anymore and not speak.

But who could speak?

NATURALLY, IT IS FINALLY TOO HARD for them to sit anywhere anymore, whereupon Dale says to Smith, "Sit, sit."

"YOOHOO, DR. DALE, DR. DALE!—so tell me, Dr. Dale, did they come and kill you yet or is it just a joke?"

"Oh, just a joke," says the herring, "just a joke."

SMITH IS WALKING ALONG and walking along and so here comes Dale, and so Dale says to Smith, "Mr. Smith, Mr. Smith, pardon me for asking you such an impersonal question, but if you would please be so good as to hasten to stultify my curiosity as to what you, as a layperson, are doing with like a one-legged chicken?"

So Smith says, "You are asking me, Smith, the multimillionaire, as to what I, Smith, the multimillionaire, am doing here with like this one-legged chicken?"

Dale says, "This, as a practitioner of medicine, is definitely along the lines of my question to you, Mr. Smith."

Smith says, "Listen, it is a long story what I am doing with what you are referring to as one-legged chicken."

Dale says, "Please, what story is not a long story?"

Smith says, "Well, first to begin with, I, Smith, go to the market the way I always go to the market and I make the purchase of this chicken. So the next thing you know, I get home with this chicken and I put it down in the kitchen, but would the chicken relax and quit it with the constant peck-peck-pecking? So suddenly I, Smith, think to myself all of a sudden what could this chicken be doing but attempting, as a chicken, to communicate with me, Smith, as regards a secret message, so naturally I start digging there in the kitchen where the chicken is giving me the message and, lo and behold, one thing leads to another and, bing bang, from the digging, guess what forty, fifty feet down happens. Because the answer is I, Smith, the layperson, hit a gusher and now I got an oil well, thanks be expressly and completely to this, God forbid it heard you, this one-legged chicken!"

Dale says, "Okay, so you got an oil well, but why, pray tell, is this chicken a one-legged chicken?"

Smith says, "Speaking to you as a medical man, what did you hear yet, you heard nothing yet, because not even a week goes by before I, Smith, the man of wealth, notice the chicken is sitting there on the telephone with a broker, so what with one thing and another, bing bang, it's the jack-pot, forget it just big money, now we are talking bucks."

Dale says, "I, the doctor, did not ask you money, Mr. Smith, I asked you the leg, what gives with the leg, Mr. Smith, being the fact this is a one-legged chicken?"

Smith says, "I explained already, I explained—so what's left to explain? This chicken which you are looking at, it sits itself down with a couple of your top investment people and the upshot is such revenue which you would need a fleet of trucks for you to get it all picked up and delivered."

Dale says, "Mr. Smith, Mr. Smith, the money is one thing—as a man of science, I did not ask you not one word about the money—what I asked you about as a man of science, is why is this chicken a one-legged chicken!"

Smith says, "You don't get it as to why this is a one-legged chicken? You are still saying to me, Smith, the layperson, you, Dr. Dale, the practitioner, still do not get it as to the one-leggedness of this chicken? Idiot!" shrieks Smith. "Imbecile!" shrieks Smith. "A chicken as wonderful as this," shrieks Smith, "so would you sit down and eat it all at once?"

SMITH GOES TO THE DOCTOR.

Smith says to the doctor, "Are you the doctor?"

Dale says, "I am the doctor."

Smith says, "Doctor, doctor, I could not for the life of me sleep no more, I, Smith, I couldn't do it!"

Dale says, "Speaking to you as my patient, Mr. Smith, so tell me, so why is it you could not sleep, pussycat?"

Smith says, "Because all night long I keep hearing wood creaking and glass cracking and an engine running."

The herring says, "So listen, darling, so if you are such a

bigshot hotshot with your hearing, then how come you do not also hear with your ears hair falling?"

Smith says, "Hey, what did you do with Dr. Dale?"

The herring says, "Who, moi?"

SMITH DOES NOT FEEL SO GOOD, so Smith goes to the doctor and he says to the doctor that he, Smith, does not feel so good, and the doctor takes a look at Smith and says to him, "Boy oh boy, it is definitely and positively finished for you, it is definitely and positively curtains for you, your goose, I got to tell you, could not be more totally positively cooked for you—so go figure two, three days still to go yet, okay?—okay, I give you three days tops to go yet, okay?— but meanwhile, so it wouldn't make you feel so bad, a person like you which thought he had his whole life stretching out for years and years ahead of him and then finds out, bing bang, God help him, he didn't, he didn't, he's a goner, he's a goner—I, Dr. Dale, as a professional, will tell you a little something which will be like a little pick-me-up for you and which will give you like a little lift for you— namely, that not two seconds ago before you paraded yourself in here, Mrs. Smith telephoned to tell me our lovely, lovely son just bought himself like a lovely new home with the nicest new lawn out back for a cow."

SMITH HAS A BROTHER who has a cat and who is crazy

about the cat and who never wants to go anywhere away on vacation because he knows he would go so crazy worrying about the cat, so Smith says to the brother for him to go and go have himself a nice vacation, whereas he, Smith, will take good care of the cat, will look after the cat, will supervise the cat, will stand at attention for the cat, will give every consideration to the cat, will hover over the cat, will be at the beck and call of the cat, will dance around the cat, will wait hand and foot on the cat, will stand on his left ear for the cat, would not for anything take his eyes off the cat.

So the brother goes away and the instant the brother gets off of the train he telephones Smith and he says to Smith, "So tell me, so how is the cat?"

And this is how Smith answers him.

Smith says to him, "It's dead, the cat."

So the brother of Smith is like in shock and he cannot even speak, he is so stunned, and it takes him whole entire minutes for him to come to his senses again and even to open his mouth to speak, but then when he finally can speak, the brother of Smith says to Smith, "You are some brother I got. Boy oh boy, I just want to tell you, you are some brother I got. I can't believe it, what a brother I got. Boy, it is some lucky thing I am here to hear it because if I was not here to hear it, I, your brother, would not believe it, what kind of a brother I got. I mean, who could ever believe it you are the kind of brother I got? I call you up on the phone, I call you, my brother, up on the phone when I just this instant just got off of the train, and I ask you like a civilized person to tell me how is the cat, and you know what you say to me? Have you any idea what you say to me? Were you listening to yourself when you just said what you said to me? Because here is what you just said to me— you said to me, bing bang, the cat is dead! So did you hear me or did you hear me, bing bang, the cat is dead? So tell me, speak to me as my brother, answer me in the context of you are my brother and I am your brother, is this or is this not what you just said to me?"

Smith says, "You heard me, the cat is dead."

The brother of Smith says, "Sure, I heard you, of course, I heard you, who could not hear you? But tell me, do you, as my brother, have even the slightest conception of how you just said it to me when you said it to me—just, bing bang, the cat is dead? I mean, let's face it, is this the way you say something like a thing like this to somebody when, number one, the individual you are addressing is your brother and, number two, the subject of the conversation is the cat you promised you would protect with your very life? I mean, think about it, I just want you to stop for a minute and think about it—is this the way you are supposed to say a thing like this or is it not? I mean, if you have any consideration for someone, if you have any feeling for someone, if you have even the least little shred of kindness and gentleness and decency in your system for someone, do you think you just turn around and say to this person, bing bang, the cat is dead? So answer me, do you or do you not, as my brother, owe me an apology? Because I, as your brother, am standing here and am listening to you and am holding the telephone and waiting like a civilized individual to hear you give me your answer."

Smith says, "Well, I could not, as your brother, just sweep the facts under the carpet and not inform you as to the fact that that's it and that's it, two seconds after you got on the train, the cat keeled over and, you know, it dropped dead."

The brother of Smith says, "Wait a minute, wait a minute, you still do not get the picture, do you? I talk to you like a civilized person, but you still do not begin to get even the first particle of the picture, do you? I mean, what is it with you, what kind of a brother did they hand me with you, I stand here holding the telephone in my hand trying to make a plain simple statement to you, but do you comprehend even the first thing which I am saying to you—which is you should make a little more effort to show a little more consideration for people's personal feelings? I mean, instead of just saying to me when I call you up and ask you how is the cat that, bing bang, the cat is dead, what you should say to me is something along the lines of like, look, here in a nutshell is what has evolved vis-à-vis with the cat since when you first got on the train—namely, I took the cat up on the roof for a little breath of air and, lo and behold, what with this, what with that, what with the other thing, it would appear the cat caught itself a little chill up there on the roof because we are noticing a mild case of the sniffles as of two, two and a half hours ago, but meanwhile we are taking every conceivable precaution and I myself have put the cat to bed and we are making absolutely certain it gets plenty of fluids and stays covered up and keeps warm and that there are no drafts coming from anywhere in the room, and then, when I called you back in a couple of hours to get an update from you on what's what with the status quo of the cat, you would say to me thank God you didn't take any chances and let the cat run around and get itself overheated or anything because, lo and behold, it sounds like there is a little cough which you can just barely detect in the chest and maybe there is like a little temperature on the order of maybe a fever which has been developing along with it, plus which the cat is looking just a tiny bit maybe logy and listless for the last twenty minutes, et cetera et cetera—so you tell me just to keep things one hundred percent on the up-and-up that you are going to telephone the doctor just to see if he thinks there is even the slightest possibility to begin thinking in terms of is there maybe like a virus somewhere in the offing. So then, when I call you back to ask you what the doctor said, you would say to me, well, the doctor has the theory it looks like a virus is maybe definitely in the picture, so just to play safe and be totally on the conservative side his advice is that we rush the cat over to the hospital and that he, the doctor himself, is going to be racing over there so they could be all set to get busy on the right battery of preliminary tests but no, no, no, not to worry about anything, that everything is totally under control, private nurses have already been arranged for on an around-the-clock basis and you are fly-ing in a top man who wrote the book on chest conditions, so then, when I get back in touch with you after that, you would say to me, look, who can always tell from one minute to the next as regards the pros and cons of medical science, things did not exactly progress along the lines all parties were anticipating, the situation took a sudden turn for the worse and, to be totally forthwith with me, it looks like the emergency head office is probably thinking in terms of going along with the analysis of downgrading the cat from guarded to critical—but meanwhile not to get myself overly excited, not to work myself into too much of an uproar, the whole situation is in a constant state of flux, the fever might be breaking any instant, so then when I checked back with you later in the night, you would say to me you yourself, as my brother, listened to the cat's chest and that you could hear like a little bubble deep down inside of there so okay, so sure, so even as a layperson, you didn't have any choice but to take it for granted there was probably some involvement of the lungs, which didn't look too good to you, but no, no, no, I should not get myself upset and aggravated, the oxygen tent and the intravenous could not be working more beautifully—okay, the vital signs are nothing to brag about but meanwhile where there is life there is hope, everything which can be done is being done, et cetera, et cetera. So then you could wait until I had a cup of coffee and then call me back on the telephone and say to me the way a brother would say to a brother, go know with medical science, not even the biggest brains could always tell with medical science, nobody could ever predict nothing one hundred and ten percent with medical science, that as of two, three minutes ago, with all parties concerned in attendance, the cat, may it rest in peace, passed, if only by the slenderest of a thread, away. So did you hear me or did you hear me when I showed you how a brother is supposed to talk to a brother and not like, bing bang, forget it, the cat is dead!"

"You're right," says Smith. "I should be ashamed of myself," says Smith. "I, Smith, should turn over a new leaf and learn to be a more considerate individual," says Smith.

"So okay, so skip it," the brother of Smith says. "I mean, let's face it," the brother of Smith says, "a cat is just a cat, right? But so meanwhile, so tell me, so how, pray tell, is Mama?" says the brother of Smith.

Smith says, "Mama?"

The brother of Smith says, "Yeah, sure, Mama—so how, I asked you, so how, pray tell, is Mama?"

Smith says, "Oh, Mama, Mama—I almost forgot— look, here in a nutshell is what has evolved vis-à-vis with Mama since when you first got on the train," says Smith. "Namely, I took Mama for a little breath of air up on the roof."

SMITH AND DALE SIT DOWN and decide they need to go get some fresh air somewhere, so they get up and they go to the woods and they are out in there in the woods and they are walking around in the woods when all of a sudden there is this feeling which Smith suddenly gets where Smith feels like there is something which is like clutching into him there on his back, like there on his back there is this terrible horrible grabbing feeling which is digging into him and clutching him back there on his back and it's like maybe a claw, a claw—but Smith is naturally too afraid to try to turn around and see if he can see what it is because Smith figures if he tries to turn around the thing, whatever the thing actually is, it would maybe suddenly start to get too overly excited all of a sudden and do something rash, like maybe even bite, so instead of Smith trying to turn around, Smith whispers to Dale, "Dr. Dale, Dr. Dale, listen, listen, do not do anything or anything like that, but just be a sweetheart and on my back you will notice that there is something back there which is like giving me, Smith, like a terrible horrible grab—like a claw, like on my back this claw—so be a sweetheart, Dr. Dale, and take a look and when you have taken your look, please, in a nice gentle calm sensible manner, please tell me, Smith, if you see something back there which could be the thing which is giving me such a terrible deep grab, please. So tell me, Dr. Dale, so do you or so do you not see something which is along the lines of what I, Smith, am referring to?"

Dale says, "Sure, I see something. How could I not see something? Who with two eyes in his head could look and not see that big as life there is something?"

Smith says, "Dr. Dale, Dr. Dale, you will notice how I, Smith, am making it my business to be absolutely careful to keep whispering. So, listen, don't forget to make sure you also don't stop whispering. So okay, so Dr. Dale, so are you all set to keep on whispering, Dr. Dale? Because I, Smith, want you to do me a favor and whisper to me what the name of it is, this thing which I, Smith, keep feeling clutching me with like this unbelievable claw like deep in my back."

Dale whispers, "What is it? You are asking me, Dale, for me to stand here and tell you what is it?"

Smith whispers, "This is my very question to you, Dr. Dale. The thing which is grabbing me such a grab, Dr. Dale—I beg you, I beg you, please tell me what is it."

Dale whispers, "Mr. Smith, Mr. Smith, please do not make me have to insult your intelligence by reminding you that I, Dr. Dale, am a physician and a general practitioner and not a, you know, a furrier."

"MR. SMITH, MR. SMITH, remember me, Mr. Smith?"

"Could I, as a layperson, ever forget you, Dr. Dale?"

"So tell me, Mr. Smith, so do you hear something, Mr. Smith? What do you hear, Mr. Smith?"

"Dr. Dale, Dr. Dale, naught but the mellowy sound of your mellowy voice, Dr. Dale."

"Mr. Smith, Mr. Smith, but you couldn't not possibly not hear it, Mr. Smith!"

"Naught, Dr. Dale."

"No moo?"

"Naught."

"No ding?"

"Naught."

"No ping?"

"Naught."

"No ha ha ha ha ha ha ha?"

"Nope."

"Nothing?"

"Only thee, Dr. Dale."

"You mean to tell me you didn't hear goodness and mercy following us all of our days, Mr. Smith?"

"So was this supposed to be also including and not skipping Thursdays, Dr. Dale?"

SMITH GOES INTO A PLACE to get himself a bowl of soup in the place and the waiter is bringing the bowl of soup to Smith and Smith suddenly notices, God in heaven, it is too unbelievable, but the waiter has got his thumb right down there in the soup, so Smith says to the waiter, "Hey, what kind of a waiter are you, you are some kind of waiter, putting your thumb down in there in my soup!"

Whereupon the waiter says to Smith, "A thousand pardons, a thousand million pardons, I am so ashamed of myself, it makes me sick for me to have admit this about myself, I don't know what got into me but I will never get over the fact I went ahead and did what I did without first stopping myself, but the thing of it is is this is such hot soup and I have such a bad infected thumb and I am so terrified that it is going to keep getting worse if I do not keep soaking it in something hot and wet every chance I can conceivably get, because, to tell you the absolute truth, I am absolutely scared to death about it that maybe I am going to have to get my thumb amputated or something because it is so totally full of such hideous fucking pus the way it is and the doctor said to me that if I do not keep soaking it every chance I get he, the doctor, Dr. Dale, as my physician, is not going to be prepared to sit down and take the responsibility onto his own professional shoulders as to what could happen to my thumb with regard to cutting it or not cutting it off—so, hey, Jesus, please forgive me, you know?—because, honest to Christ, it's fucking killing me, I am in absolute fucking devastating agony from it, whereas like I really need the money, you know?—so I mean like how in the world could I, just a waiter, like not come in to work?"

Smith shrieks, Smith screams, "Are you fucking crazy— pus, agony, amputation! Are you fucking out of your fucking mind in my fucking soup—pus, agony, amputation!"

Pleads the waiter, "Please God that you will find it in your heart of hearts to please forgive me, sir."

"What please forgive!" shrieks Smith. "Where please forgive!" shrieks Smith. "Who please forgive!" shrieks Smith.

"I am down to you on bended knee," pleads the waiter.

"Bended!" shrieks Smith. "Knee!" shrieks Smith. "Madman, moron, idiot, ignoramus—my advice to you and to your fucking thumb is that you should go ahead and stick it up your fucking tookis if you are so interested in keeping it hot and wet and not cut off and amputated!"

"Please, please," begs the waiter. "I know," begs the waiter. "But I swear it to you, sir, this is just exactly what I was doing in the kitchen before they said I had to come out here and bring you your soup!" begs the waiter.

SMITH GOES TO THE DOCTOR.

Smith says to the doctor, "Are you the doctor?"

The doctor says, "I am the doctor."

Smith says, "Doctor, doctor, I got a worm."

Dale says, "You got a worm?"

Smith says, "I got a worm."

Dale says, "Take down your pants and let me listen."

So Smith takes down his pants, and Dale puts his ear to the rectum of Smith and listens and says to Smith, "In my medical opinion, you maybe could get from it milk and butter and maybe like an interesting color of cream."

"MR. SMITH?"

"Dr. Dale."

"You still don't, as a layman, hear nothing fishy?"

"Like what, Dr. Dale?"

"Like an engine, Mr. Smith."

"Like an engine going ping ping ping ping?"

"Like an engine like that, Mr. Smith."

"Uh uh."

"Or ding ding ding ding?"

"Nope, I couldn't help you, Dr. Dale, nothing but you as a general practitioner, this is all that I, Mr. Smith, hear—plus like maybe also the rumble of the pages turning."

"Mr. Smith, Mr. Smith, you say you hear the thunder of the pages turning, Mr. Smith?"

"So far just a rumble, Dr. Dale—when it's thunder, when it turns to thunder, believe me, from me, Smith, you will hear an indication, Dr. Dale—I promise you, I as your patient would not deprive you of my screams."

DALE IS SO HAPPY to see his old friend Smith, Dale cannot believe it that after all of these years he is bumping into his old friend Smith, Dale is beside himself with happiness and excitement because of the coincidence of bumping into his old friend Smith, so Dale gives Smith a tremendous smack on the back and screams, "Smith! Smith! My God, I am so happy to see you, Smith!" whereupon the little boy that Dale has knocked down shrieks, "Mommy, Mommy, the man hit me!" and suddenly it all of a sudden dawns on Dale that if it really was Smith which was lying there shrieking, then would not Smith be as purply as Dale is?

"BIRDS, MR. SMITH?"

"Ixnay, Dr. Dale, please, definitely, Dr. Dale, no birds, please, neither, Dr. Dale."

"No, I mean a joke about birds, Mr. Smith."

"Oh, a joke about birds, Dr. Dale!"

"Exactly, Mr. Smith!"

"Why, I thought you'd never ask, Dr. Dale! You have been so down in the doldrums for pages and pages, Dr. Dale!"

"Mr. Smith, Mr. Smith, shall we therefore, as I as your doctor and as you as my patient, not shoulder our burden and just get on with it, Mr. Smith?"

"Birds, Dr. Dale! Excellent, Dr. Dale! Would I, as the layman, be surmising with all due precision if I were to prognosticate it was two birds which you have in mind, Dr. Dale, counting, as a practitioner, in round numbers?"

"Two birds it is, indeed, Mr. Smith. Two birds which have not laid eyes on each other in years and years and years, Mr. Smith. But so one day they happen to bump into each other and they cannot believe it how happy it makes them to suddenly for them to see each other, it is wonderful how happy it makes them to all of a sudden for them to see each other—so, lo and behold, they spend the whole day together going around all over the place together and they have the absolute time of their lives together, so when sundown finally rolls around and day is done and so forth and so on, the first bird says to the second bird, 'Look, this is really crazy, it was so great being together again, it's totally nuts for us not to keep doing this on a regular weekly basis, so what do you say to the proposition that we get together like this on a once-a-week basis like this starting next week on the 9th, then going from there to the 16th, and then from there to the 23rd, et cetera, et cetera?'

"'Great, great, great!' says the second bird, 'I really think that's a great idea,' says the second bird, 'let's decide to meet right here on this same branch next week, on the 9th, at let us say as birds at nine sharp!' says the second bird.

"'Terrific!' says the first bird, 'just terrific—this branch, the 9th—not the 8th, not the 10th, but the 9th at nine o'clock on the dot—so who could not remember it, 9 and nine, or nine and 9, numerals notwithstanding?'

"So, okay," says Dale, "the 9th rolls around and there the first bird is, there on the very branch where it was all set up for the two birds to meet, but nine o'clock comes and goes, and then so does nine-thirty, whereas, hold it, hold it, is the second bird anywhere in sight? Because the answer is forget it, nowhere is the second bird anywhere to be seen! But so by and by it goes from ten to twelve to three o'clock, and then, bing bang, one thing leads to another until, my God, it is almost time for the sun to go out of the sky and for it to get too cold for a bird to be out in the world anymore, when guess what, guess what—here comes the second bird and the first bird sees him coming and he shouts to him, 'Hey, some bird you are, some bird you are, here I am, just the way we had planned, just the way we had both stood here and agreed, so here was me, waiting right here on this very branch from first thing this morning, and yet where were you, were you here where I was, were you anywhere in the vicinity of where I was? Oh, but so now look, now look, it is time for us to have to go back home now and so, sure, sure, so now you show up!—God, the crust on you—Christ, you really are some bird!'

"Whereupon guess what the second bird says to the first bird, Mr. Smith," says Dale.

Smith says to Dale, he says to him, 'It was such a nice day, I thought I'd walk'?

"No," says Dale, "you are forgetting in your mind what day I said to you as a medical man it was."

"Oh," says Smith, "in that case this—'Honest to God, I'm sorry, I'm sorry, but what with the horrible weather, can you blame me for being too scared for me to fly?'"

"Merci croissant, Mr. Smith."

"Beaucoup bouffant to you too, Dr. Dale."

SMITH AND DALE SIT DOWN and decide to go for a walk, so they get up and go out for a walk and they are walking along and they are walking along when, bing bang, Smith and Dale meet a man who is carrying a bird.

So Dale says to the man, "As a general practitioner, my question to you is this—so why are you carrying this bird?"

The man says, "The reason I am carrying this bird is to save it from being eaten by the herrings."

Smith says, "But, hold it, hold it, herrings do not eat birds! Since when do herrings eat birds?"

Dale says, "Mr. Smith is right, Mr. Smith is right—herrings, I never heard of them eating birds!"

So the man with the bird says to Smith and Dale, "Listen, they'll eat if they want, they won't if they don't."

"AND VICE VERSA DITTO," says the bird.

SMITH AND DALE SIT THEMSELVES DOWN and decide to go out for a walk and Smith and Dale get up and go out for a walk and it starts pouring, it starts coming down like cats and dogs, it has not rained like this since who knows when, never in all of their born days have Smith and Dale ever been in a situation where the rain was anything like this, so Smith opens up his umbrella up but, lo and behold, the umbrella is nothing but holes, the rain comes running right down through all of the holes, so Dale starts shrieking, he is shrieking and shrieking at Smith, "What kind of an idiot are you! What kind of an imbecile are you! What kind of an ignoramus are you! Who ever heard of a moron who comes outside out-of-doors with an umbrella which has in it nothing but holes when you open it up?"

Says Smith, "Answering you as a civilized individual, Dr. Dale, please tell me, pray tell, how I, Smith, was supposed to know as a layman it was going to rain?"

THE SMITHS AND DALES are all set up on the ship and are on board on the ship lifting all of the goblets to their lips and lifting all of the caviar to their lips when, lo and behold, they hear there is this tremendous pounding there on the door, and so notice when Dale goes to the door to open the door, look at the look on Dale's face when Dale goes to open the door—it is all smiles, the man is all smiles, the wonderful drama of the pounding on the door—oh, imagine it, imagine it, the boundless possibility of the bounding main, the ineluctable theater of the piratical brain!

"MR. SMITH?"

"Dr. Dale?"

"So tell me if you could stand it for you to hear maybe one more one, Mr. Smith?"

"Better another one and another one and yet another one, Dr. Dale, than in place of another one instead nothing at all."

"Mr. Smith, Mr. Smith, speaking to you as a man of science, Mr. Smith, these words which you are infiltrating to me are the words of a genius, Mr. Smith."

"Credit where credit is due, Dr. Dale—or did you not take yourself a good gander at the completely brilliant incredible creature which is writing us this book?"

"Mr. Smith, Mr. Smith, addressing you as the lay-factor between us, my advice to you is be smart, don't look."

"With all due respect to you as a general practitioner, Dr. Dale, the man, please pay attention, is one of us."

"Yet be this as it may, Mr. Smith, don't make me have to sit here and tell you a joke is a joke, but a book is a book."

"Speaking of which, I, Smith, trust you couldn't help but notice, Dr. Dale, that I, as the layperson, have been waiting here with all due patience aforethought, Dr. Dale, while meanwhile also in a state in highest expectations that you, as a professional man, would please be so good as, with the new joke, to wax forthcoming."

"Mr. Smith, Mr. Smith, a thousand sincerest heartfelt pardons—believe me, I, as a man of medicine, couldn't be more apologetic to you on a bet—so, listen, the situation which is vis-à-vis the joke is this—you-know-who is meanwhile up there nailed up there on the stick, whereas them, the fellows which did or didn't do it, depending on your version, they are down there let us say just sitting around down there passing like the time. So what is it, three, four of these fellas? So anyway, what else do they have to do with themselves, do they have anything else to do? So the answer is forget it, they figure to themselves they got nothing better to do, so to make a long story short, they decide in their minds they will hang around there in the vicinity of the hill to like see what's what, maybe there will be like something they could notice. So it is already hours and hours, when all of a sudden there is suddenly like this calling and calling coming from up on the stick from you-know-who. So, my God, they could not believe it, the man is still going up there, it's fantastic, it's incredible, the man is in such a terrible situation up there, but meanwhile, listen, listen, the man is actually calling from up there—so, bing bang, one of the fellas calls back up to him and says to him, 'Hey, what is it, what is it?' Whereupon guess what the answer is, Mr. Smith. So could you guess?"

Says Smith, "I, Smith, have to admit it to you, Dr. Dale, that as a layman I could not even begin to formulate for you not even the smallest modicum of an educated guess."

Dale says, "So you maybe think he is asking for like water maybe? Or maybe like somebody should come up to him and try to like resituate one of the nails?"

Smith says, "Who, pray tell, would know? Would I as a layman know? I, Smith, am thinking and thinking, but to be totally forthwith with you as a physician, Dr. Dale, so who would even know where to start?"

Dale says, "So here is the answer. So the answer is this. So what the fellow nailed up there says is this—he says 'Hey, I just wanted to tell you fellas I can see the roof of my cousin's new house from up here.'"

MRS. SMITH RUNS OUT into the street shrieking and screaming, "Spare the children, spare the children, dear God in heaven, couldn't you at least make them give some consideration to maybe sparing the children!"

Suddenly there is all of a sudden a lot of lightning and thundering and here is what God answers the woman.

He says to her, "Show business is show business."

SMITH SAYS TO DALE, "We got to stop it with the wise-cracks, we got to quit it with the wisecracks, we got to cash it in with the wisecracks, we got to call it a day with the wisecracks, we got to forget it with the wisecracks, we got to learn to live without the wisecracks, we got to skip it with the wisecracks, we got to put it to bed with the wisecracks, we got to sweep it under the carpet with the wisecracks, we got to think twice with the wisecracks, we got to throw in the towel with the wisecracks, where will it ever get us for us to keep spritzing and spritzing with the wisecracks?"

Dale says to Smith, "But so like so where will it ever get us if, you know, if we don't?"

DALE'S GRANDSON is going to have a bar mitzvah, so Dale goes and gets the caterer on the telephone and Dale says to the caterer, Dale says, "Listen, I know I do not have to tell you that this is Dale the medical man speaking, and that I therefore could not conceivably begin to consider a bar mitzvah where it is like every Tom, Dick, and Harry's grandson's bar mitzvah—so do I make myself clear to you or do I make myself clear to you? In other words," Dale says to the caterer, "the caliber of bar mitzvah which I, as a medical man, am waiting to hear you, as the expert, draw a picture of for me would naturally be a bar mitzvah which it would drive the whole Smith family totally crazy when they hear about it that I, Dr. Dale, had the taste and the wherewithal to set it up for my grandchild, God love him, because this is how exclusive and classy the whole situation is going to have to be for me right from one end of it to the other. So talking to me as a professional person, what, pray tell, is your professional proposition to me?"

The caterer says to Dale, "Dr. Dale, Dr. Dale, as an unquestionable professional person yourself, not to mention naturally also as the grandfather of the grandchild, what would you say to the idea of like a cattle-car bar mitzvah?"

Dale says, "A cattle-car bar mitzvah?" Dale says, "You are talking to me as the grandfather of the grandchild as to like a, you know, like a cattle-car bar mitzvah?" Dale says, "Because even as a man of science, I got to admit it to you I never heard of a cattle-car bar mitzvah."

The caterer says, "Sure, you never heard of a cattle-car bar mitzvah, Dr. Dale! I am not surprised to hear it that you never heard of a cattle-car bar mitzvah, Dr. Dale! Name me anybody yet who is so in on the inside up there with the inside upper-level people that they have already heard already of a cattle-car bar mitzvah, Dr. Dale! Because you know what, Dr. Dale? Because you want for me to tell you what, Dr. Dale? Because the answer is that you and yours would be the very first upper-level people on the list, Dr. Dale—because this, Dr. Dale, is how completely how very très it is, a function like a cattle-car bar mitzvah!"

So Dale says to the caterer, "I like it, I like it—so speaking to you in your capacity as the caterer, please be so good as to do me the courtesy of recuperating to me the various different particulars as regards the nature of a cattle-car bar mitzvah per se, given that I, the doctor, give you my personal guarantee I am listening and am weighing all sides of the argument pro and con from all advantages."

The caterer says, "Well, first of all, the question is who ever did it before, did anybody ever?"

Dale says, "Good, good—so far, so good."

The caterer says, "Second of all, will anyone in their right mind believe it even when they see it?"

Dale says, "Wonderful, wonderful—I got to really hand it to you, this sounds really to me as a doctor terrific."

The caterer says, "Third of all, whoever lives through it, would they ever even begin to be able to think for the rest of their life about anything else?"

Dale says, "Marvelous, marvelous—bing bang, a cattle-car bar mitzvah, I love it, I just love it!"

The caterer says, "Whereas you naturally understand, Dr. Dale, the asphyxia will be exorbitant."

Dale says, "What exorbitant! Who exorbitant! Where exorbitant!" Dale says, "Listen, darling, for Dale's grandchild, you think Dale would think to stoop to stint on the question of hot versus cold hors d'oeuvres?"

SMITH'S WHOLE ENTIRE SYSTEM just had such a shock that Smith's whole entire system decides it could not begin to take it no more and so Smith keels over and gets in his bed and is getting ready to pass away and so then Mrs.

Smith comes to him to say her goodbyes to him, and so after Mrs. Smith has said her goodbyes to him, Smith says to Mrs. Smith, "Look, sweetheart, bride of brides, our whole life long our married life long did I, your husband, ever once, as your husband, ask of you anything which you wouldn't like a sweet adorable pussycat hurry up and give? Because the answer to this question, as I, Smith, your husband, do not have to lie here on my deathbed to tell you, is skip it, forget it, you, as my bride of brides, could not come running fast enough to do it. So listen to me, sweetheart, are these the facts or are these the facts? In other words, this is why I, Smith, in consideration of the situation here at this stage of the game, have to lie here on my deathbed and be perfectly honest with you as your husband when I ask you if you could just take two seconds and give me a nice quick blow-job before I pass away. So what is your opinion, you could or could not do it in consideration of the situation I never once asked you, as your beloved, for you to do it before as of this particular stage in the lifetime game?"

So Mrs. Smith goes ahead and does it, whereupon all of a sudden Smith suddenly makes the most miraculous of recoveries, throwing off the bedclothes and vaulting out of bed, but then the next thing you know, would Mrs. Smith stop standing there shrieking and screaming?

The answer is no, the woman would not do it.

So Smith says to her what, what—what is this woman

jumping up and down and making such a terrible tumult about, does the woman not realize what just happened was a miracle, does the woman not recognize what a miracle looks like when the woman sees a miracle, how come the woman does not know she should instead be down on her knees to God thanking God instead?

Mrs. Smith says, "What recognize! Who recognize! Where recognize!" Mrs. Smith says, "It's just I suddenly just thought to myself I could also probably have taken two seconds and saved Roosevelt."

SMITH HAS TO GET BACK into his deathbed again and so Smith goes and gets into it and lies back and closes his eyes and is waiting for God to come take him when all of a sudden, lo and behold, Smith suddenly sniffs the most gorgeous smell of something and so he hurries up and he opens up his eyes and he sits back up in the bed and he whispers to the child who is sitting there, Smith whispers to the boy, Smith says, "Look, I, your father, want you to know I could not possibly be more knowledgeable of the fact of what a sweet son you are, coming here to me to my deathside like this and sitting with me here while I have been in the midst of the course of my waiting here for God to finally come and get me. In other words, sweetheart, do not think for one tiny minute I, your father, do not totally appreciate it in my heart of hearts as to what a gorgeous sweetheart you are, just sitting here from one minute to the next with nothing to do but twiddle your thumbs while I, Smith, wouldn't have to do anything but lie back in the bed, whereas you, as my son, got to all by yourself go through the heartache of like the vigil, on the one hand, not to mention also the deathwatch on the other. So ask yourself, darling, am I, your father, expressing myself with crystal clarity on this subject or am I expressing myself with crystal clarity on this subject? But so meanwhile, sweetie, be this as it may, I want for you as my son to be completely comprehensive of the fact that I, as your father, could not help but just an instant ago to notice was a certain particular like a smell of something which I could nevertheless detect flat on my back here in my deathbed like a dying man in my nose. So, tell me, sweetheart darling, speaking in words of one syllable to you, I, your father, am asking you the question of is your wonderful mother in the kitchen maybe making chopped liver?"

So the son of Smith says to Smith, "Yeah, Daddy— Mama is in the kitchen making chopped liver, Daddy."

So Smith says, "Cutie boy, pussycat, I, as the dying individual, realize I would not have to point out the fact to you as the person which is keeping the deathwatch, let alone who is also maintaining the vigil, that figuring it even at the outside, I, as your father, got, let us say, maybe only two, three minutes left to go yet tops, absolutely tops—so, honey sweetie, cutie sweetie, be a sweet darling and go run to the kitchen and like advise your wonderful mother she should hurry up and give you like on a spoon a little quick taste of the chopped liver for me, your father, before God comes and I couldn't lie here and look him in the face and say to him for him to wait for one more instant more."

The son of Smith says to Smith, "But it's like for after, Daddy—Mama's making it for after."

ALL OF THE CHILDREN are in the school sitting at their little desks in the school and the teacher gets up and she says to the children that it is milk time, that it is time for all of the children to get out their little cartons of milk and to drink their milk, so all of the children take out their little cartons of milk and they all put their nice crisp drinking straws into their little cartons of milk and all of the children are all drinking their milk when all of a sudden the teacher suddenly notices that there is a child back there in the back of the room who is not drinking his milk, so the teacher says to the child, she says, "Sweetheart, drink your milk."

Whereupon the child answers the teacher this way.

He says to her, "Go ahead and forget it! I would not sit and drink the goddamn milk if you paid me!"

So because the child's mother is dead and because the child's father is dead and because all of the child's sisters and brothers and cousins and aunts and uncles are all of them also dead and because there is nobody in the whole wide world but the child's grandmother and grandfather who are some-one in the child's family which got away with not being

dead, the teacher says to the child for him to bring the grandmother to the school when the child comes to the school the
next day—so, bing bang, the grandmother comes and, lo and
behold, guess who the grandmother is, because, thank God,
God love her, it is Mrs. Smith, and the teacher says to her,
"Mrs. Smith, Mrs. Smith, I, as the teacher of your grandchild, want you to please pay attention to this, Mrs. Smith,"
whereupon the teacher says to the children it is milk time,
that it is time for all of them to get out their little cartons of
milk and to put their nice new crisp fresh drinking straws in
and to drink their lovely milk, and so all of the little children
get busy doing every little thing which the teacher has just
said, but back there in the back of the room, the same child,
the same child, would he even budge one inch?

Because the answer is no, he wouldn't do it!

So the teacher says to him, "Sweetheart, darling, I want
for you to be a nice good little boy and for you to please put
your straw in and drink your milk."

The child says, "Enough already with the goddamn milk!
I would not drink the goddamn milk! Bitch, bitch, you can
shove it up your ass with the goddamn milk!"

So the teacher turns to Mrs. Smith and the teacher says
to Mrs. Smith, "Mrs. Smith, Mrs. Smith, did you just hear
what your grandchild just said to me, Mrs. Smith?"

Mrs. Smith says, "I heard him, so fuck him."

ALL OF THE CHILDREN are in the school sitting at their little desks in the school and the teacher gets up and she says to the children it is milk time, that it is time for all of the children to get out their little cartons of milk and to drink their milk, so all of the children take out their little cartons of milk and they all put their nice crisp drinking straws into their little cartons of milk and all of the children are all drinking their milk when all of a sudden the teacher suddenly notices there is a child back there in the back who is not drinking his milk, so the teacher says to the child, she says to him, "Sweetheart, please drink your milk."

But the child cannot drink anymore or sit anymore or speak anymore or even just anymore not have the energy not to either anymore neither.

ALL OF THE CHILDREN are in the school sitting at their little desks in the school and the teacher gets up and she says to the children that it is milk time, that it is time for all of the children to get out their little cartons of milk and to drink their milk, so all of the children take out their cartons of milk and they all put their nice crisp drinking straws down into the cartons of milk and all of the children are all drinking the milk when all of a sudden the teacher suddenly notices there is no mouth, there is no room, the corner is running around the corner, the bird is shrieking moo.

"SO DIDN'T I TELL YOU, MR. SMITH?"

"So didn't you tell me what, Dr. Dale?"

"That it wouldn't be such a good idea for you to turn your back on the bigshot which went ahead and set himself up as the boss of this particular book."

"Dr. Dale, Dr. Dale, do I or do I not reinterpret you right when I say to you that you are saying to me that it is better to swim headfirst into a whole school of pickled herring than for you to set foot inside of a single non-referential sentence?"

"Mr. Smith, Mr. Smith, speaking to you along the lines of the particular hyperthyroid which you just had the courtesy to edify for me as a layman, what choice, as a medical man, do you stand there and leave me, Mr. Smith, except to stand here and say to you touché, Mr. Smith, touché?"

"Déjà vu, Dr. Dale, déjà vu to you too, Dr. Dale."

THIS TIME IT IS naturally Dale who has to go get into his deathbed. So Dale is in there in his deathbed and is waiting for God to come down to him from heaven to him so that he can meet his maker, but meanwhile can the man find any peace of mind to just be left alone for two seconds so that he can just lie there as a physician and concentrate on the general nature of the contemplation?

Because the answer is no, he couldn't do it!

This is because, God love him, there is a son which is sitting there at the bedside of Dale's deathbed and the boy keeps constantly nuddering Dale, poking at him with his fingers and waking Dale up and making Dale open up his eyes so as to get Dale to favor him with like the distillation of his, you know, of his wisdom—so finally Dale like hints with his eyes for the boy to pay attention, pay attention, look, look, notice, notice, there is a glass of water which is sitting right there, there on the night table.

So the son of Dale says, "What is it, Pop? What are you trying to tell me, Pop? Are you trying to communicate to me something about this glass of water here, Pop?"

"Yes, yes, yes," says Dale, "the glass of water," says Dale, his voice the feeblest whisper.

"So what about it?" says the son of Dale.

"Here, here, give me," says Dale.

So the son of Dale puts the glass of water in Dale's hand, and Dale says, "My son, my son—listen, my son—always drink from here, from over here on this side over here, yes?"

So the son says, "That's it? That's the wisdom? Always drink from the side which is there next to where your lips are? Shit, Pop, you lie here and call this wisdom?"

Dale says, "Idiot, moron, ignoramus—you drink from over on the other side over there which is the opposite of where your lips are, imbecile, yutz, you tell me you can't see what happens with the fucking water?"

"YOOHOO, DR. DALE!"

"You are maybe yoohooing to me as regards to the answer to a certain riddle, Mr. Smith?"

"Dr. Dale, Dr. Dale, my answer to you as to the riddle,

Dr. Dale, is riddle, shmiddle, Dr. Dale—whereas my statement to you as to yoohooing to you is as follows, Dr. Dale—is it or is it not conceivably the case that you, as a man of modern science, are possibly giving too big of a discount to the fact that this here is like strictly an auditory situation which we as individuals are finding ourselves situated with here—meaning as far as the joke we just heard, who could begin to figure it out when the joke got in it like a certain proverbial visual element of the water spilling down?"

"Mr. Smith, Mr. Smith, do I or do I not understand you to be standing there and calling into question the fact of like would there or would there not be an adequately sufficient enough context with reference to the wrong side of the glass of like water and so on and so forth?"

"Dr. Dale, Dr. Dale, this is what I, Smith, with all due reference to you in theory, am calling into question."

"In other words, Mr. Smith, what you are saying to me as a doctor is if they could not with their own two eyes see it, then would they with their own minds get it?"

"Dr. Dale, Dr. Dale, to quote to you from the encyclopedia of simple ordinary intelligence, a fool is soon parted from his patience, sight gags not exempted."

"Mr. Smith, Mr. Smith, to quote to you from my own brain, who is the layman, is it you or is it you?"

"Op cit, Dr. Dale—I admit it, concierge and op cit."

MR. AND MRS. SMITH ARE OLD AND SICK. There is just no telling how old and how sick Mr. and Mrs. Smith are. Nobody probably has any idea of how old and of how sick Mr. and Mrs. Smith are, probably not even they themselves have even the first idea. But so, lo and behold, so one day they show up in the divorce court and they say to the judge who is the judge in the divorce court for him to quick grant them as the Smiths a divorce.

So the judge says to them, "What divorce! Who divorce! Where divorce!" The judge says to them, "You want I should grant you a divorce?" The judge says to them, "Just out of curiosity, enlighten me as the judge, you have been married in married matrimony to each other for how many years by now—sixty, seventy, what?"

Mr. and Mrs. Smith say, "Judge, in round numbers, the number of years comes to sixty-eight last month."

The judge says to them, "Sixty-eight years?" The judge says to them, "You have been man and wife for a total of sixty-eight years!" The judge says to them, "For sixty-eight years you have been man and wife and now, as man and wife, you are telling me that you are coming to me, as the judge, for you to get like a divorce?"

So Mr. and Mrs. Smith say to him, "So what is your opinion, judge, you think enough is never enough?"

THEY COME TO SMITH and they say to Smith would he or would he not be willing to be the judge of a certain argument. So Smith says to them, what are the ins and outs of the argumentation in this argument? So the three men of God who this particular situation has reference to here in this argument, the three of them sit themselves down and they say to Smith that the argument is to argue what the nature of good is, that this is the subject of the argument. So Smith says to them who would not be interested in being the judge of such a high-class argument, what an honor and a privilege for him it is for him to be the judge of such a high-class argument, go ahead, argue the argument, they could count on Smith as the perfect individual who would sit and listen and tell them who wins and who did not win when they get to the end of the argument.

So the first individual speaks and he says, "Speaking to you as a rabbi, my opinion is this—piety, piety, piety, period! In other words, a man says his prayers, this is good—the rest, whatever it is, you could pick it up and go stick it in the trash and walk away and forget about it!"

Whereupon the second individual says, "Listen, my esteemed colleague definitely got a point of view and I for one wouldn't be the one to sit here and spit on it, but meanwhile I also wouldn't give you two cents for it neither! In other words, whereas insofar as the nature of good is concerned, speaking to you as a rabbi just as much as he just did but, notice, notice, also as a rabbi which just so happens to happen to have a brain in his head, the answer is good, the answer is that the nature of good, is your interpersonal relations! Look at it this way—you got people, so you got to get along with them! This is why I say to you a person which gets along with their interpersonal relations, this is the person with a good nature—whereas the rest of them, skip it, the whole gang of them, they could turn around and make you vomit!"

So then the third individual says, "Who couldn't sit here and not have plenty of reason for being so wonderfully proud of themselves for sitting here with two such brilliant individuals as these two wonderful rabbis, whose words of wisdom, I, as a rabbi myself, don't have to tell you, are like a symphony of music to my own two ears. Geniuses, these men are complete geniuses, take it or leave it! And you know what I say? Let me tell you what I say. I say thank God we still got in the world geniuses along the lines of these two brilliant individuals which you just heard sitting here expressing themselves to you so that you wouldn't be left unknowledgeable as to their heartfelt opinions, because I, as a third party, can, in all sincerity, tell you who in their right minds would want to live so quick in a world which didn't have such fantastic geniuses like them sitting here in it! So did everybody hear me or did everybody hear me?"

There is an outburst of applause—but Smith swiftly gestures in a fashion which is magisterially juridical and order, thank God, is instantly, you know, restored.

Whereupon the third individual continues in his statement as follows—"I, on the other hand, however, couldn't

help but to come to a totally different twist on it with reference to the question of what is the nature—or let us say
the structure—of the situation vis-à-vis good, my conclusion being that what we are thinking in terms of when we
think in terms of good is when, lo and behold, the breath-
taking creature which is employed in the capacity of she is
the new social director as regards your house of worship,
this creature says to you yeah, sure, she wouldn't give you
any more arguments anymore, she would be delighted and
thrilled to accompany you in the capacity of as your com-
panion for a weekend somewhere nice, please God the sun
should only be shining and there would be a nice lovely situation as to the quality of the beach and the pool, not to
mention there should also be an outlet in the vicinity for
superlatively high-toned cuisine—and so off you go to the
most exclusive of hotel establishments like two brand-new
lovebirds which couldn't wait to get there and check in
with each other in their most sumptuous of accommodations—so naturally, vis-à-vis the shtupping, there is first
and foremost a little acquaintanceship along the lines of this
department, then you go put on like your beach togs or
your pool togs, whichever you are most comfortable in and
are willing to go participate in accordingly, and then you
come back up to the room and have some more shtupping
before you put on your dining togs and go out and sit yourselves down to a perfectly lovely arrangement with regard
to the subject of supper, so then when you have eaten

absolutely your last wonderful mouthful and could not even begin to stuff in one more luscious morsel, then you go take a taxi back to your accommodations and what with one thing leading to another, it is all of a sudden time for you to have some more shtupping together again—so then when you wake up in the bed the next day, the whole next day turns out to be just like the day you just had except for the fact that this time there is at least two, three times more shtupping than there was the day before—whereupon, lo and behold, the morning of the next morning after that morning, before you got to both of you hurry up to get packed up and go back home again, she comes and gives you a nice quick blow-job and meanwhile swears to you she would first personally sit herself down and take poison before she would ever even think to breathe one single solitary word with reference to the companionship which you have been having with her to another living person. Therefore I say to you that it is this, gentlemen—if I may address you in the capacity of an individual who has spent his life extending all due consideration to this woefully inadequate subject—which like constitutes my theory as to what is the nature of good! So yes or no, do I, in your opinion, win the argument or do I win the argument?"

"Mr. Smith, Mr. Smith!" shriek the other two men of God, leaping to their feet in terrible outrage. "Hey, wait a minute, one second here, Mr. Smith!" the other two men of God stand there screaming at Smith, "Because the question which is on the table is what, pray tell, is the nature of good, not what is the nature of terrific!"

SMITH AND MRS. SMITH MAKE UP their minds to go take a nice trip somewhere together—so, lo and behold, there they are in their fabulous setup as it relates to the stateroom which they are occupying, when Mrs. Smith, who has been standing regarding herself in the mirror, breathes a sigh of terrible anguish and says, "So tell me, pussycat, what is your honest theory per se, darling, is it your personal analysis we are contemplating an occasion where I, Mrs. Smith, should be ruminating principally along the lines of the cerise pantsuit with the shirred flounce and the fuchsia lucite pumps, meanwhile coming to the conclusion of the emeralds both as to the necklace question plus also as to the situation vis-à-vis earrings, or would it in your one hundred percent candid opinion make more sense for me to probably compromise in terms of the plain brocade backless with possibly a sporty assortment of the two beaded sweaters if I carried the turquoise one on my arm in the elevator and switched a certain number of items as mainly concerns bracelets and so forth over to the other arm so that all you would not see until I sat myself down and could get myself relaxed was maybe only my diamond self-winding by Mr. Leo?"

Smith says, "Beloved person, speaking to you in the context of in case you did not hear it when I said it to you in the context of for the first time, breakfast, according to the shipboard notification, they would not keep serving down there forever."

MRS. DALE GOES TO THE DELICATESSEN and she says to the man behind the counter of the delicatessen, she says to him, "Be a nice sweet darling person and be so good as to start slicing me some nice lean brisket, ennui?"

So the man behind the counter of the delicatessen gets out the brisket and starts slicing it and when the man has sliced some brisket, he stops and says to Mrs. Dale, "Keep going?"

Whereupon Mrs. Dale says to the man, "Sure, sure, keep going. Did I tell you not to keep going?"

So the man keeps slicing the brisket and when he has sliced many more slices of brisket, he says to Mrs. Dale, "Having a little game of rummy this afternoon for the girls, yes, Mrs. Dale?" He says, "Listen, Mrs. Dale, when I get finished slicing you this brisket, Mrs. Dale, maybe I could also cut you some nice lean pastrami too?" He says, "So tell me, Mrs. Dale, does this or does this not look like enough brisket for you or should I just keep on going, Mrs. Dale?"

Mrs. Dale says, "Yeah, keep going, keep going."

So the man behind the counter of the delicatessen keeps slicing and slicing and he says to her, "Boy oh boy, Mrs. Dale, let's face it, it looks like you and the doctor are having a very substantial get-together, yes?" He says, "Listen, dear lady, maybe you should start thinking in terms of like a platter, yes?" He says, "So with regard to the subject of an assortment, Mrs. Dale, I got here also, don't forget, salami, tongue, turkey, pastrami, corned beef, yes?" He says, "So this is some major affair you and the doctor are putting together, yes?" He says, "All seriousness aside, Mrs. Dale, we are talking in terms of a real function, yes?" The man says, "But so look, Mrs. Dale, do you want me to keep going here with the brisket, or would you instead prefer for us to begin like, as individuals do business, evaluating the other tempting possibilities?"

Mrs. Dale says, "Keep going."

So the man behind the counter of the delicatessen keeps on slicing slices of brisket and he says to her, "So who is kidding who, we are talking about a wedding or about a bar mitzvah, Mrs. Dale?" He says, "So taking me into your confidence, which is it, Mrs. Dale, it's a wedding or it's a bar mitzvah?" He says, "Mrs. Dale, you are or you are not aware of the fact that I am in a position to take care of my big customers as regards competitive terms with reference to certain rentals—namely, we are talking in terms of chairs, dishes, tablecloths, not to mention a little three-piece orchestra which would be headlining with kings and queens if they still had enough of them to make a serious market for real musicians." He says, "So do you want me to sit down and start figuring a contract and the various different discounts and write-offs, Mrs. Dale, or do you want for me to keep going?"

Mrs. Dale says, "Keep going."

He says, "Lights, Mrs. Dale, lights! God in heaven, so

tell me, what in the world is wrong with me I didn't mention already lights!" He says, "Will somebody please stop and tell me what could have conceivably gotten into me to stand here like a lunatic and not to mention already lights!" He says, "All seriousness aside, Mrs. Dale, I must be totally out of my mind just to stand here slicing and slicing and slicing and not to think to myself moron, idiot, colored lights, colored lights, like these wonderful lights which would wink on and wink off for who else but for the doctor himself, God love him, the physician, plus for Mrs. Dale, the wife of the practitioner and the man of science!"

"Hold it!" shrieks Mrs. Dale, indicating with a nod of her head the slice of brisket which the man behind the counter of the delicatessen has just this instant finished slicing. "That's it! That one there!" screams Mrs. Dale.

MRS. DALE HEARS THE TELEPHONE and goes and gets the telephone and says into the telephone, "So hello?"

The herring screams, "So you are sitting thinking we as herrings were too busy swimming?"

MRS. DALE HEARS THE TELEPHONE again and goes and gets the telephone again and says into the telephone again, "So again and again hello?"

The herring screams, "Kike, kike—the fucking brisket!"

THE TELEPHONE STARTS RINGING AGAIN as soon as Mrs. Dale has put down the telephone again, so Mrs. Dale picks up the telephone again and Mrs. Dale says into the telephone again, "So one more time hello?"

The Farmer in the Dell says, "Get ready to suck it!"

DALE COMES HOME and goes and sits in the kitchen and gets out his newspaper and starts reading his newspaper and is reading and reading his newspaper when all of a sudden Dale suddenly begins to smell something which, as a man of medicine and science, would Dale not know what it is?

SMITH COMES HOME and goes and sits in the kitchen and gets out the newspaper and is sitting in the kitchen with the newspaper when in comes Mrs. Smith and as the wife of Smith she says to Smith, "Downstairs."

So Smith puts down the newspaper and goes downstairs.

SMITH GOES TO THE DOCTOR and says to the doctor, "So speaking as Smith, are you the doctor?"

Dale says, "I am the doctor, I am the doctor, what could I, Dr. Dale, the doctor, be but the doctor?"

Smith says, "Doctor, doctor, I don't feel so good, I don't feel so good, so tell me as a doctor what is wrong!"

Dale says, "I, the doctor, shall hasten to make a medical examination of your body if you will partake with me of the amenities of my own personal examining room."

So Dale examines Smith and says to Smith, "Mr. Smith, Mr. Smith, speaking to you in the capacity of my role as a general practitioner, I, Dr. Dale, have no alternative but to ask you—did or did you not ever entrain for Banbury Cross?"

DALE HEARS THEY JUST PUT IN a new golf course in the vicinity, so Dale goes over there to the new golf course and he says to them there at the golf course, "Look, who has time to stand here with you anymore as a doctor with you anymore and beat around the mulberry bush with you? So getting right to the red tape with you, so could you or couldn't you hide me here in a hole?"

They answer him.

They say to him, "Regarding the witticism with specific reference to the fucking brisket."

They say to him, "You are standing in a dell."

They say to him, "Jack from Jill plays here."

They say to him, "Also the whole family Horner."

DALE IS WALKING ALONG and walking along and he sees a girl who is a nice-looking girl who also is just walking along and walking along. So Dale says to the girl, "Such a nice-looking girl like you are, so tell me, pray tell, so what are you doing just walking along?"

The girl says, "What?"

Dale says to the girl, "I said, such a nice-looking girl like you are, so what are you doing just walking along?"

The girl says, "I'm sorry, I didn't hear you."

Dale says, "What are you doing just walking along and walking along like this, is there perhaps, addressing you as a medical man, maybe a possible medical reason?"

The girl says, "A reason, a reason."

SO DALE GOES TO THE MAN who makes the clothes and Dale says to the man who makes the clothes, "My name is Dr. Dale, the chap of up-to-the-minute medical science."

The man who makes the clothes says, "It is a blessing, such a blessing, we have at least science."

"DR. DALE?"

"Mr. Smith?"

"Are you the doctor, Dr. Dale?"

"This is another riddle, Mr. Smith?"

THE TELEPHONE RINGS.

The telephone rings.

Mrs. Smith does not answer the telephone.

Mrs. Smith does not go pick up the telephone.

Mrs. Smith just stands there and looks at the telephone.

So Jack says to himself, "I am going to go over there and go fuck out her kike brains for her and then go cut the kike open from head to kikey toe."

BUT NOT TO SELL A JACK SHORT.

Because the man even figures out something which he could probably do afterwards with his dingus to her toe.

SMITH GOES OVER TO THE STATIONMASTER and Smith says to the stationmaster, "Pardon me, young man, but could you please do me the courtesy, please, of please informing me, please, as to when it is which the next departure from here will be leaving here from this particular station?"

The stationmaster says, "Soon, soon—the whole world will be boarding at this station soon."

SMITH READS IT IN THE NEWSPAPER that it is a good idea for him not to read anything in the newspaper—but before Smith can stop reading it in the newspaper, they come and make him read it in it some more and some more.

DALE HEARS ON THE TRAIN Smith shrieking on the train like a man shrieking on the train.

Like this.

"Oh, God, I am spitting cotton! Oh, God, am I, Smith, spitting cotton! My God, my God, my God, this time I, Smith, am really and truly actually spitting cotton!"

So Dale listens to Smith shriek on the train. Then when they get off of it, Dale listens to Smith shriek off of it.

SMITH GOES TO THE DOCTOR and Smith says to the doctor, "Doctor, doctor, are you the doctor?"

Dale says, "For the sake of conversation, well and good, you, Smith, be the patient and I, Dale, will be the doctor."

Smith says, "Doctor, doctor, here comes another sight gag."

Dale says, "Oy gevalt, my diagnosis is the train, the train, you took the train to Banbury Cross!"

MRS. SMITH IS SITTING EATING with a spoon some soup when in comes Mrs. Dale shrieking, "Bitch, bitch, where did you get in a spoon any soup?"

MRS. SMITH SAYS TO MRS. DALE, "So tell me, Mrs. Dale, do you and the doctor have a mutual spoon?"

MRS. DALE GOES OUTSIDE and screams, "The children, is there no relief for even for the children?"

Jack screams back at her, "We're thinking book rights, dinners at the White House, medals from the Swedes!"

MRS. SMITH GOES OUTSIDE and screams, "Guess what, guess what! It's the same inside as outside!"

MRS. DALE HAS A MARRIED DAUGHTER and the married daughter has a child and Mrs. Dale says to the married daughter, "Look, be smart, take my advice, let go of the child and let the child come with me."

So Mrs. Dale tries to take the child, and the married daughter, she lets go and lets her take it.

SOME PEOPLE ARE CARRYING DALE and somebody says to Mrs. Dale, "Mrs. Dale, Mrs. Dale, what a terrible thing the doctor cannot walk, Mrs. Dale."

Mrs. Dale says, "The doctor cannot walk."

MRS. SMITH HEARS a telephone ring and she says to herself, "What ring! Who ring! Where ring!"

DALE HEARS DALE SAY, "It's not moi."

THE LITTLE WINDOW OPENS and the man says, "Yes?"

There is a voice.

A person is answering.

The person says, "Your whole religion would not believe it what they stand there and make me do to people."

SMITH RACES UP TO THE MAN who is the guard and Smith shrieks to the man who is the guard, Smith shrieks, "The man's mother! The mother's daughter! The daughter's father! The father's child! The child's apostrophe! The apostrophe when they use instead the genitive!"

THE WOMAN SAYS, "But you do not understand yet. He does not understand yet. There is nobody who understands yet. Just drink it, just drink what's in the milk."

JILL SAYS, "Jack?"

THERE IS SUDDENLY such a lightning and a thundering.

"WONDERFUL, SO WONDERFUL, SO WONDERFUL," says Dale, winking a big purple wink to Smith, whereupon the gigantic vicious naked person gives Dale a gigantic vicious naked grab and fucks Dale up the ass with this gigantic vicious naked prick of his.

THE WOMAN CANNOT GO pick it up and stop it from its ringing because it's ringing, ringing, ringing.

THE VOICE SAYS, "But what are you telling me for?"
    The voice says, "Shouldn't you be telling somebody else?"
    The voice says, "Go tell somebody else."

SMITH IS SITTING READING and in comes Mrs. Smith and Mrs. Smith says to him, "Smith, Smith, Smith."

LIKE CLOCKWORK, for food, Smith and Dale get their food. So one day they decide to eat instead a piece of shit.
    But there is not a piece to eat.

DALE SEES MRS. DALE all stretched out with not one stitch of anything on her.
    She's—Mrs. Dale is—more empurpled than she is—this Mrs. Dale—as a person, purplescent.

HORNER.

Nimble.

Sprat.

Quick.

Leave taken via beanstalk.

SMITH GOES TO THE DOCTOR.

Smith screams, "Doctor, doctor, are you the doctor!"

Dale says, "Doctor, doctor, am I the doctor?"

Smith screams, "Doctor, doctor, help me, doctor—I, Smith, as Smith, am dripping and dripping!"

Dale says, "Listen, Mr. Smith, I, as the doctor, would not want to stand here and kid with you—because according to my diagnosis of you as a doctor, you wouldn't get away with just only just dripping and dripping. Speaking to you as the person who is my patient, I would have to say to you that it definitely looks to me more along the lines of instead dripping and dripping and dripping and dripping and dripping and dripping and dripping."

"OVEN!" shrieks Smith.

"In the oven!" shrieks Smith.

"So this is a figure of speech?" shrieks Smith.

"NEVER ONCE DID HE in his finery utter even one fire-fangled word!" shrieks Mrs. Smith.

"JACK?"

"Jill?"

"You ever hear the one about what do they do with the rest of the matzo after they use the balls in the soup?"

"No, Jill. I did not hear that one, Jill. So how does it go, Jill? I would like to hear how it goes, Jill."

SMITH AND DALE GO LOOKING for a fish. Dale keeps on not finding a fish. No one ever saw anything like it, the way it is always Dale who is the one who is looking for a fish, whereas Smith, he is the one who keeps forgetting what they are looking for looks like, a fish or not a fish.

DALE IS ON THE TRAIN and Smith is on the train and everybody is on the train and they are all shrieking for God to come get them off the train, please get them off the train, but is there one of them who stops and thinks it's probably the same God who, if he's God, stuck them on it?

All of a sudden there is such a terrific lightning and thundering—whereupon, lo and behold, God speaks.

HE SAYS, "I can't see anything from up here."

HE SAYS, "I can't hear anything from up here."

HE SAYS, "Pardon me, but do I look Jewish?"

SMITH AND DALE ARE SITTING ON A BENCH. From first thing to last thing Smith and Dale just sit there on the bench, not wanting for them to have anything of themselves move anymore or even anymore just have it anymore.

The cold keeps meanwhile getting colder.

One of them thinks he thinks something.

Then he thinks he probably didn't.

Then he thinks is he Smith or is he Dale or is he Jack or is he Jill or, you know, is he?

DALE SAYS TO SMITH, "Doctor, doctor, speaking to you as a general practitioner, please, doctor, you got to help me, doctor, you got to be merciful, please!"

Smith says to Dale, "It was thick. It was a dilly. It was right outside there right outside the window. Green."

SMITH SAYS, "Listen, listen, because I, Smith, am address-ing you in the context of there is no context but forget it, who needs a context?—so listen, listen, if I go ahead and see if I could maybe really eat it, would it or wouldn't it be worse for me than if I didn't? Because in all seriousness, I couldn't not do nothing, pot pourri? I mean, doctor, doc-tor, you heard of betwixt and between or you heard of betwixt and between? So answering me as a layman, what, pray tell, is your opinion per se? So is it your opinion I could or could not do it—or is it your opinion do not ask?"

Dale says, "Even with my whole arms I could not fit around it to climb it, not even with my whole arms and legs."

SMITH SAYS, "If I eat half, will you eat half?"

Dale says, "The wishing well, the carousel."

SMITH AND DALE ARE SITTING ON THE BENCH. All day long they just sit on the bench. Finally, the light is gone and it is too cold anymore for them to sit in the cold anymore. So Smith and Dale sit on the bench.

SMITH SAYS, "Listen, listen, you know something which is too fantastic for words?"

Dale says, "What is too fantastic for words? Tell me what is too fantastic for words. I, Dale, could not wait to hear it from you what is too fantastic for words."

Smith says, "My whole life long I always knew it even from before it was my life yet."

SMITH GETS UP AND DROPS HIS PANTS and looks to see if any came out.

Dale says, "You want a second opinion? I will give you a second opinion. Save your breath."

MRS. SMITH AND MRS. DALE are sitting on the bench.

Mrs. Smith says, "Mrs. Dale, Mrs. Dale, so what is your opinion of the general situation, Mrs. Dale, would you have an opinion as to the general situation, Mrs. Dale, please share with me your opinion as to the general situation, Mrs. Dale, I need to know what you are thinking vis-à-vis the general situation, Mrs. Dale, I do not think I am going to be able to sit here and stand it if you do not speak to me as to what is your opinion of the general situation, Mrs. Dale, I beg you not to withhold from me your opinion as to the general situation, Mrs. Dale, I beg you, I beseech you, please not to not tell me your thinking as to the general, God help us, situation, Mrs. Dale."

Mrs. Dale says, "Don't you hear the bench? Listen to the bench. Pay attention to the bench. There is nothing for anybody to know but to know the mind of the bench."

SMITH SAYS, "Look, you will please be a nice sweet fellow, please, and you will please, quick go get for me, a nice piece of anything, please God it should only come loose."

Then he keeps squeezing until he cannot keep on squeezing anymore—or keep on squatting anymore—or keep from fainting anymore—nor from slipping back down onto Dale—nor from letting go all of the way and slipping back down all of the way back down onto, you know, Dale.

SMITH AND DALE DECIDE in their minds for them to go sit themselves down and write a book about themselves.

So could they do it?

The answer is no, they could not do it!

But neither could you, fuckface!

SMITH IS WALKING ALONG and walking along and, lo and behold, he bumps into Dale, and Dale says to Smith,

"Mr. Smith, Mr. Smith, as regards that which, as a man of science, I could not help but notice you got there in your hand—so, listen, talking to me as a layperson, is it some of it or is it all of it or is it even it in the first place?"

SMITH GOES CRAWLING ALONG and goes crawling along and, bing bang, Smith bumps into Dale.

Look at this—Smith & Dale.

SMITH IS LYING THERE as a layperson, laid out half on Dale or half off Dale, depending, as is said in science, on your perspective. But there is no perspective. Nor any science. There is Jack in the Box. Plus an ampersand.

SMITH DOES NOT FEEL SO GOOD, so Smith goes and whispers it to Dale, whereupon Dale shrieks to Smith: "Let's face it! We got to face it! Together we could maybe begin as beginners to face it! Because neither of us could keep on sitting here as doctor and as layperson and just keep on sweeping the facts under the carpet and not face it! Because what carpet? Because where carpet? Because who carpet? Don't go look to no carpet! There is no more room no more for nothing to get it in under any carpet anymore! Show me a carpet! Who could see a carpet! Forget it with the constant, constant carpet! This is why I am talking to you from the perspective of I am the one who is talking to you! So listen! Skip it! It's curtains! It's water which you would not get to come back over the dam anymore even if you stood on your left ear and begged it to do it! Your goose could not be more cooked! The fat is in the fire! Also, pay attention, the whole meat. What is not in the fire just did not come to its senses yet for it to realize where it was! But meanwhile how could it not give you a little lift when I, Dale, speaking to you not only as a general practitioner but also from past experience, make you the prophecy that geniuses will come, that complete geniuses will come, that they will be one after the other nothing but the most unbelievably brilliant geniuses which will come—listen to me, geniuses upon geniuses which wouldn't, even as geniuses, be able to sit themselves down fast enough to write such gorgeous, gorgeous books about you and yours. But so you did or you didn't hear me as the doctor, ingenue or ingenue?"

SMITH HAS A BROTHER who has a cat, so Smith goes and kills the brother and eats the cat.

The son of Smith thinks, "If Smith drops dead from eating the cat, then I, the son of Smith, will eat Smith and then eat the brother of Smith."

So he gets his hands under his cheek to make a pillow with his hands for his cheek.

He watches Smith.

He keeps his eyes on Smith.

"Smith is my father," the son of Smith thinks.

He watches him eat.

So does Jack in the Box.

IT'S A MIRACLE!

Dale suddenly vaults right up. The man just suddenly sits right up and vaults right up.

Smith says, "Look at you—bigshot, bigshot, with the all of a sudden vaulting and vaulting!"

Dale says, "Sure, vaulting! Why not vaulting? Believe me, I, Dale, the medical fellow, am definitely vaulting!"

Smith says, "Yes, yes, but what is the nature of this impetuous, you know, like this impetuous vaulting?"

Dale says, "Hey, you think God would pick me as the person to get his shvantz into without me first exhibiting like a little like extra initiative?"

"JACK?"

"Jill?"

"Did you ever hear the one about how come is it that they have the highest death rate when the top death rate is one death per every person?"

"No, Jill. I did not hear that one, Jill. How does that one go, Jill? Can you tell me how that one goes?"

SMITH IS ON THE TRAIN.

Dale is on the train.

Who is not on the train?

Is even the stationmaster not on the train?

It is only God, the jerk, which missed the train.

So much for chasing what—a hat, a cap, who knows?

WHEREUPON THERE IS all of a sudden such a lightning and such a thundering—and such a lightning and such a thundering—and such a lightning and such a thundering— which in due course subsides—and then which goes and subsides some more—and then which ebbs away—ebbing completely into complete ebbness and whichness.

SMITH AND DALE DECIDE to go to the woods and so they go to the woods and they are going through the woods when suddenly Smith all of a sudden feels on his back like a grab, like the most terrible horrible ghastliest grab.

Smith does not shriek, does not scream, does not whisper to Dale for Dale to tell him what it is. Smith knows what it is. Who does not know what it is? It is what it is. It is what it was always to be.

THERE IS A TREMENDOUS POUNDING at the door.

"So speaking to you from the standpoint of the laity speaking to the non-laity, so do we, as two persons, go open it or do we go open it?" says Smith.

"Let's for laughs go open it," says Dale.

ALL OF THE CHILDREN ARE ALL OF THEM THERE.

AN ENGINE GOES PING.

IT GOES PING PING.

IT KEEPS GOING PING SOME MORE.

IT GOES PING PING PING PING PING.

BOY OH BOY, IS THIS AN ENGINE GOING PING!

DALE IS CRAWLING ALONG and crawling along when, bing bang, what do you know, Dale bumps into Smith. So Dale says to Smith, "Mr. Smith, Mr. Smith, so speaking to you as Dr. Dale, what, pray tell, are you doing crawling along as a layman with only a half-eaten hand in your hand?"

SO THE SON SAYS, "Are you trying to tell me something about the water? It looks to me like you are trying to tell me something about the water. So what are you trying to tell me about the water? You keep acting like you are trying to tell me something about the water. So which is it, which is it—it's acting or it's actink?"

Dale says, "Yes, yes, water."

The son says, "So what about it, what about the water?"

Dale says, "I beg you, I beg you, water."

"HEY, JACK!"

"Hey, Jack!"

"Hey, Jack!"

[YEAH, SURE, SO OKAY, so there should have been six of them in all, sure—Quick, Box, Sprat—plus Horner and Nimble and Beanstalk. But so, hey, listen, who could keep them straight? You think you couled keep them straight? You know what? The answer is you couldn't do it!]

THEY COME TO SMITH and they ask Smith for him to be the judge of an argument, and so Smith says to them for them to tell him what is the nature of the argument—so they say to Smith the nature of it is which is worse as to pings, the ping you hear first or the ping you hear last?

Smith says to them, "Be smart and listen instead to a certain bird which I could mention to you which, fluent in languages, never even opened its mouth."

SO THEY GO ASK DALE the same question, and Dale says to them, "Look, let's face it, what choice do you give me as a professional man save but to ask you what your own various different opinions as far as being laypersons are?"

So one of them says, "I would personally have to go along with the theory of the first ping being worse."

So then another one of them says, "Sure, sure, I myself could detect the legitimacy of this philosophy, but when it comes to my own opinion, I beg to diverge with what he just said and promulgate instead the analysis that it is definitely and absolutely no question but the last."

So Dale says to them, "I even as a doctor could not

myself completely believe it, but let us not kid ourselves, I got to go along with the argumentation of the both of you like a total of one hundred and ten percent."

Whereupon Smith shrieks, "Hey, hey, wait a minute, wait a minute—fake, fake, what kind of a fake are you?— the bigshot, the practitioner, the man of science!—to sit there and make such a moronic statement to people who come to you to ask you to be the judge of something, telling these two ignoramuses the both of them are right when you know perfectly well the both of them could not possibly both be right when it is a mathematical impossibility for the both of them both to be right!"

Dale says, "My God, it's a miracle, it is definitely the most amazing miracle!—you also who just said what you just said, you too, Smith, you're also right!"

MRS. DALE SAYS, "Sure, keep going, why shouldn't you keep going, what's to stop you from keeping going, could I stop you from keeping going, could anyone stop you from keeping going, would even God stoop to stop you from keeping going? So which is it, the keeping or the going?"

DALE SAYS, "Addressing everybody as a man with a practice, my advice to you is for you first to first eat from first between them as regards first the toes!"

SMITH SAYS, "Taking your advice as a layman would take

it, this could or couldn't be legitimately in your mouth when you also got in it kaka which is begat from milk?"

MRS. DALE SCREAMS, "Yoohoo! Oh, yoohoo to everybody! Expressing myself as the practitioner's bride, watch out from the book writer, you could die from the book writer!"

MRS. SMITH SAYS, "So tell me, darlings, when they make the movie, you think a Yid would or wouldn't play the cow?"

THE DIRECTOR SAYS, "Amazing, it is simply amazing—I mean, how do you people do it?"

"It's actink," say Smith and Dale.

THERE IS SUDDENLY all of a sudden a sudden pounding as of a pounding on a door.

MRS. SMITH SAYS, "Listen, don't kid yourself so fast, so who would not be wordless, turning and turning to such a beautiful indescribable crisp!"

IT IS THE POUNDING that's pounding.

It is the pounding of the pounding.

So Smith says, "Do we go open it or do we go open it?"

Dale says, "What would you say to this as a secondary proposition? We go and like, you know, like open it."

TO SIT ON WOOD, they sit on wood.

SMITH SAYS, "I could never get it through my head what day it is all day today, or was it?"

DALE SAYS, "So is this including you couldn't if even if it wasn't, for instance, a, you know, a Thursday?"

IT IS NOT DARK. It is not cold.
  It is not anything.
  Anyway, ping, ding, so long as you got your health.

SMITH SHRIEKS, "Dr. Dale, Dr. Dale, do me a favor and don't forget not to move a muscle, Dr. Dale!"

WHO EVER HEARD such a pounding as of in pounding?

DID THE WORLD EVER HEAR?

SO SMITH AND DALE GO OPEN THE DOOR.

WHEREUPON, BING BANG!
  Lo and behold!

"THAT ONE, THAT ONE THERE!" all the laypeople shriek for them to see like such sport.

A LADY, WHAT A LADY!

O WHITE, WHITE!

JESUS FUCKING CHRIST, on a farkakt white horse!

HERE COMES A QUOTE FROM SMITH & DALE.

"WHAT DINGS? WHO DINGS? Where dings? But could you sit there and deny the woman full credit for a tintinnabulation or could you sit there and deny the woman full credit for a—fuck it, fuck it—forget it!"

MERRY, MERRY—bells, she has bells!

O WHO HAS NOT HEARD THEM, the bells on her toes!

SECOND NOTE

They are dead.

I thought I could keep myself from trying to find out, but the answer is I couldn't do it. So I went ahead and made inquiries. I telephoned the Friars Club. You know what I mean when I say to you the Friars Club? Anyway, whoever it was who got on the line said, "Oh, them, the two of them—they're dead." When I was asked why it was I was asking for the lowdown on an act as ancient as Smith & Dale, I said the reason why I was doing it was by way of my wanting to do a little last-minute favor for my dad.

Here is what was said after that:

"Was he in the business?"

"I'm sorry?"

"In the show business—your father, is your father, you know, retired from the show business?"

"Oh, sure—yes, I think he's pretty retired from it now."

"Hey, that's great—so what was the billing of his act?"

"Phillie Lish—he worked under the name Phillie Lish—but it was Filip Liskowitz before it was that."

"Never heard of it, Lish or Liskowitz—but you tell your dad Smith and Dale had themselves laid out side by side, okay? Oh, and wait a sec—make sure you say the stone says 'Booked Solid.' All the old-timers always get such a big incredible kick out of it when anybody ever tells them that."

I think I should call back sometime and see what the Friars say the story is with respect to Jenny Wren. Granted, Jenny Wren was nowhere near the headliner Rose La Rose or Lili St. Cyr was. But when it comes to your living legends, hey, you can't tell me Jenny Wren was not Miss Jenny Wren.

Ist die Kuh
schon über den Mond
gesprungen?
—THE FARMER IN THE DELL